REDEEMER

Stefanie Dawn

Redeemer
Elements of Abduction
Book 3

Stefanie Dawn

This book is a work of fiction. Any references to real events, real people, and real places are used fictitiously. Other names, characters, places and incidents are products of the Author's imagination and any resemblance to persons, living or dead, actual events, organizations or places is entirely coincidental.

Disclaimer: The material in this book contains graphic language and sexual content and is intended for mature audiences, ages 18 and older.

ISBN: 978-1763870505

Editing and Proofing by Swish Design & Editing
Book Design by Swish Design & Editing
Cover Design by Eric at
The Book Brander
Published by Angels and Fire Books
Cover Image Copyright 2024

DEDICATION

To all those who question their sanity for not
only falling in love with a fictional character but a
monster or an alien no less.
This is for you.

REDEEMER

CHAPTER

I

LANIR

My brother and I predicted that one day, the Ghaal would again get hold of the females they'd been seeking this past decade—the humans. Since they found the species were genetically compatible with them for breeding, they wouldn't give up. The Moeks—interstellar transporters willing to kidnap innocent species from other planets and galaxies for a price—had finally come through, returning with four of the females the Ghaal sought.

But my brothers and I couldn't let the Ghaal have them.

The Ghaal was a violent species, having almost entirely wiped themselves out through war. Those who remained on the planet after most of the population left to seek another solar system to inhabit, fought desperately to solve the infertility issues created by years of chemical warfare. As the generations went on, their numbers dwindled further, along with specialists in technology and science, leaving them with broken and outdated technology and forcing them to survive more and more on the basics alone. Their experiments took out many of their remaining females as the Ghaal's desperation increased.

A scientist's final act was creating my brothers and me—synthetic organisms, intelligent, able to adapt, to change gender, and to breed.

But we chose not to help the Ghaal.

They were not a species worth saving.

They tortured us, once again trying to solve their issues with violence, until we found a way to escape, fighting our way free under the constant threat of annihilation from the one weapon the Ghaal held against us.

They created us.

They could destroy us just as easily.

After the failed experiment that was our lives, the Ghaal hired transporters and then pirates to abduct females from other planets, and my brothers and I spread across the continent. We were determined to rescue as many innocent lives as we could and steer them away from the Ghaal colony. If we couldn't stop the abductions, the least we could do was make sure as many beings as possible were safe on this planet, equipped to survive, and aware of the location of the Ghaal colony and the dangers they posed.

Eventually, the Ghaal found what they'd been looking for—human females could be used for breeding to help bring them back from the brink of extinction. But they were reckless and too enthusiastic, and in their desperation to confirm pregnancies and compatibility with dwindling technology, they had resorted to surgical means to do so. The females in their possession were killed in the Ghaal's desperate and rash attempts.

So, they sought more.

We had hoped being cut off from the intergalactic trade meant they wouldn't find them, but there were always pirates willing to bend their morals for a price.

Head tilted toward the sky, I watched as four units were dropped from the transporters' ship.

Four, not six, which was odd.

The Ghaal, beyond being violent and abhorrent, were superstitious about numbers—they always worked in sixes. If they were willing to break this rule, then their desperation had reached new levels. If they could only get four of the females and were still willing to proceed with the plan, then they would become unpredictable, and more of a threat than they already were.

While it seemed a small thing, it had been a superstition they had held on to with more reverence than they treated each other.

A unit fell near my cave home, and I trekked up the mountain toward where it landed.

As it opened and the small female peeked out, her expression terrified and yellow hair falling in front of her face, I knew she was the same as the species the Ghaal had been searching for.

She was my second chance.

My chance to redeem my failures for the one I hadn't been able to save.

I must protect her.

At any cost.

CHAPTER 2

SAMARA

Abducted.

Why me? Why did they choose *me?*

Was it because I live alone? If my boyfriend, Dylan, and I hadn't broken up three weeks ago, would the aliens have left me alone? If I had a dog, maybe? Or several cats? Or a snake? If I didn't live on the top floor of the apartment building where they could reach me through the roof, would they still have chosen someone else?

I knew I'd never get answers, but the questions still flew around in my mind as though if I asked them to myself enough times, I could pull an answer from somewhere in the depths of my psyche. The other girls abducted didn't seem so concerned with *why them*, which was odd to me. Doesn't everyone want to know *why* to almost everything in life? *Why* do people do the things we do? *Why* are we here? *Why* are we drawn to some people more than others through an inexplicable force? *Why* do we bond with a person as though we loved them before we've even met?

Call me foolish, but I always loved the idea of soulmates.

Although as I was pulled into an alien spaceship—even with my usual attempt to stay positive and remember a grander force was watching over me, remnants from a strict religious upbringing that I had picked and chosen which elements I still wanted in my life—I had to admit my chances of finding my soulmate were being dashed into nothing.

Being removed from planet Earth puts a stickler in any plans.

But I tried, Lord knows I tried to remain positive. It was hard.

The aliens who'd taken me kept three other women and me on their ship for a week and a bit, or maybe several weeks, I honestly couldn't be sure. The days started to blur into each other after a while. Following an initial probing—not like *that,* thankfully, but in my mouth and against my belly button—the aliens had left us alone, only coming to our cages to feed us a couple of times a day. They never spoke, not that we would've understood them anyway, and after a failed escape attempt, their contact with us was even more limited. So, I started to wonder if maybe they weren't so bad. They outnumbered us twenty to one yet never tried to hurt us. Even after we tried to escape—I wasn't keen on the flimsy plan in the first place, but all the other women were determined to try, and it seemed foolish to stay behind if, by some miracle, they succeeded—our captors didn't get violent with us.

Our alien kidnappers kept us fed and our waste buckets clean, so while we were technically prisoners, it felt more like we were being treated as... *cargo.*

I couldn't decide if that was a good thing or not. Maybe good because it couldn't allow us to be damaged, but bad whenever I thought about what this meant when it came to wherever we were heading.

The other women and I could only communicate by breathing on the clear sides of our respective cages and hastily writing a word or two. I tried to communicate my thoughts on the aliens potentially being friendly to the other girls, and they would look at me with some sympathetic look as if to say, *oh sweetie, don't be so naïve.*

I'm not stupid. I knew we were in trouble, but there had to be some hope somewhere, right? They hadn't killed us when they easily could have, I'm sure. Surely, that was a good sign? While I couldn't hold the tears at bay forever—sometimes I too cried myself to sleep—I refused to wallow in it forever. But every time I tried to convey anything positive to the other girls, they would shut me down or exchange significant looks with each other. Unable to talk at length, I couldn't be sure what they thought of me, but I'm certain the word *naïve* would pop up in their lexicon somewhere when it came to me. Maybe I was, but was it such a bad thing to look at the world every day as if it were a blessing? This is the hand we were dealt. And while it was far from ideal, if we could find a way to survive, maybe we could be happy in our new home together.

Even my hope began to dwindle, and time went by slowly, the days merging into one long, agonizing wait for something to happen.

Then one day the food didn't come.

The routine was broken.

Something was happening.

Unfortunately, it turned out to be more probing. I was separated from the other girls, and the probing became more vicious and intense this time. My belly button piercing was partially ripped from my skin with how ruthlessly they poked and prodded with their cold instruments, but they didn't care. The only thing that snapped the aliens out of whatever duty they were performing was when they cut open my sweatpants and underwear at the crotch and stared hard between my legs.

I wanted to scream at them—it was humiliating and terrifying—but instead, I stayed still and hoped they wouldn't touch me more.

Then, all at once, I was ushered from the examination room and out into a hallway. The other girls were there, and no one knew what was happening. Were we being sent home? We didn't know. Everything happened so quickly. One minute, we were being probed, and the next, we were shoved into small, separate pods, which turned out to be escape pods and were shot out the side of the spaceship. I screamed until my throat was raw as the pod tumbled around, trying to catch a glimpse of where we were being dropped.

When the planet came into view, for a brief moment, I hoped it was home.

But it wasn't Earth.

The landscape was unfamiliar, the continents different, the sun too orange and large. I plummeted to this strange planet with my hands clasped, praying for the first time in many years.

My pod landed with an uncomfortable jolt despite the parachute that had been deployed. I'd seen the other pods disappear over the horizon and the mountain, and my stomach twisted into knots at the idea I was abandoned on a strange planet, alone.

I used to go camping with my parents, but not like this—nothing close to this.

The door to the pod slid open without any provocation from me, and tentatively, I looked out.

Not sure what to expect, but hoping for the best, nonetheless.

What could be worse than landing alone on a strange mountain on an alien planet with small pools of bubbling and hissing lava dotted around?

The mountain was a dappling of purple and gray, and if I peeked out of the pod and craned my neck, I could see the mountain extended far into the clouds, harsh and jagged rock that sloped down in a great sweep before leveling out into some uneven giant rock staircase. I'd landed on a flat part, but if I exited the escape pod, I'd have to navigate over pools of lava, around an unfamiliar terrain, toward where I could see the mountain leveled out further. Into the distance on one side was an ocean, although a muddy gray color, and on the other, woodlands of some sort, further to maybe a forest—a never-ending nature reserve as far as I could see. There were no cities, roads, or towns, not even something to indicate a village with a small line of smoke above the tree line.

Nothing.

I'd simply need to start walking and hope I came across someone who could help.

Steeling myself, I released my grip from the side of the pod, unaware I'd been gripping it so hard until I flexed my fingers.

Okay, Samara, you can do this.

No.

I can't.

I can't do this.

I'm frightened.

What's the use in trying to pretend otherwise? Despite my efforts to keep positive, there's a big chunk inside me telling me to simply give up and die here. Because even *if* I can get out of this pod and away from the lava pits safely, then what? Wander the planet until I find one of the other girls or get eaten by a monster?

Reality sucks, and right now, it was sucking any hope I had out of me.

Maybe someone, somewhere, had seen the pods fall and would come to offer help.

Maybe the pod that fell over the other side of this mountain wasn't so far away after all, and one of the girls would come and find me.

Maybe I'd be waiting a mighty long time for someone to rescue me.

Settling back into the small, uncomfortable seat in the pod, I drew my knees up to my chest and intertwined my fingers around the front of my shins. If I tried not to focus on the lava pits around—not an easy task—and took some deep, even breaths, I could appreciate that this place, wherever it was, was quite beautiful. I must be up relatively high because even as the mountain stepped its way down toward woodlands, I could see the landscape laid out in front of me, a brilliant display of nature, color, and life.

The sun was high in the sky, a bright orange that made me shield my eyes if I turned toward it. I could see the ocean, a sickly gray—yuck—but still, it was an ocean. Something that was familiar, and I was happy for that right now. There was a woodland with what I could assume were trees sparsely spread out over an almost sandy soil. The sand was also gray but dappled with white. Some areas were patchy while, in other spots, the two colors of sandy soil were blended in a pleasant pattern. I wondered if it was soft or gravelly.

If I ever moved from this pod and made it down the side of the mountain, maybe I could find out.

I couldn't stay tucked up here forever.

But as a cool breeze moved across the mountain from the ocean, brushing against my arms and toes,

I let it calm me and gave myself time to think as I breathed in deep lungfuls of air. The air was so fresh. I'd never experienced anything like it in the city.

Think—what would I need when I got out of this pod?

Food. Water. Shelter.

I wiggled my toes in the breeze. Shoes, I would probably need shoes too. *Better stop off at the nearest mall.* I giggled slightly and sighed again, feeling more like *myself.* I leaned back a bit and settled further into the seat.

For now, I simply needed the moment to relax. My stomach was stinging where my piercing had been ripped, and my mouth was dry. But until I cleared my head of negative and distracting thoughts, any move would be a mistake.

Closing my eyes, I focused on my breathing and the cool breeze, wishing it were home.

CHAPTER 3

LANIR

It seemed blood had a very distinct smell, regardless of the species or planet of origin.

The sickly, coppery scent invaded my nostrils and drew me around the side of the mountain, where I met my brother, Ilk, also drawn by the scent. A Ghaal was carrying a corpse, and when he dumped the body on the ground, a snarl rose in my throat.

Two small breasts on her chest and yellow hair that fell across her shoulders splayed out across the rocky ground, caked in blood. Red, instead of the greenish-gray of mine, but unmistakeably blood. Her helpless body had no fur elsewhere, except for a small tuft between her legs, and she had been cut up and sewn back together through the Ghaal's experimentation, her lifeless eyes milky white and staring.

Ilk wanted to question the Ghaal, but I couldn't wait any longer. I lifted my fist and drove it into his skull as I pinned him under me, the Ghaal's head cracked against the hard rock of the mountain. I did it again and again, cursing him internally for what they had done to this poor female and who knew how many more before her. I hated them for what they did to my brothers and me and the violence in their blood that led them to the destruction of their own species.

All my rage lasted only a handful of punches before the Ghaal's skull was in pieces, surrounded by the pulp of his head under my fist.

Ilk's face was mostly unreadable at my reaction to the Ghaal's few words—revealing to us this female was compatible with them for breeding, and they would seek more of the same species to use the way they wanted to use us.

Ilk didn't approve of my violent outburst. That much was clear. "Violence is not the answer," he chastised me.

My eyes narrowed as I stood. "Violence is the only thing they understand."

The poor, innocent female with her yellow hair lay on the ground, and Ilk and I decided to give her a proper burial. We stood by her makeshift grave, and Ilk said, "They'll find a way to get more of these females."

I knew that. I knew what the Ghaal were capable of more than most. I'd suffered at their hands as they used me as an example to show their cruelty knew no bounds. They would find a way to get more females of this species, no matter how long it took.

But when they did, I would be there to protect them this time.

The female's body we had found all those years ago, the memories came back to me now, along with the scent of blood that invaded my nostrils so sharply it felt real and not simply a memory. The female we found, caked in blood and sliced up, had the same yellow hair as the female in the unit dropped by the transporters right near where I lived.

The female in this pod would be afraid of me, but I didn't have time to concern myself with that. Nothing was more important than keeping her out of the Ghaals' hands.

This female was mine to take care of. Even if she feared and hated me, I wouldn't let the Ghaal take her. I wouldn't let her yellow hair become caked in blood the way the other female's had. I wouldn't let her be caged, experimented on, and cut up.

So, while she'd be afraid of me and the threat I potentially posed to her, I knew what was best, even if she didn't understand that yet.

She was mine to protect.

Working my way up the side of the mountain toward the unit, I kept out of her sight. If she saw me approaching, it would only make it worse for her. There was nothing I could do to stop her from fearing me to start—once she saw me, she'd immediately be frightened—so better I take her quickly and get her to safety, then we can figure out communication. I was many times larger than her. I was sure my hand could wrap around her neck, and my fingers would touch at the back.

When I was right underneath the unit, caught between two rocky outcrops, the breeze shifted, and a wave of her scent washed over me. I backed against the rocky wall of the mountain. Beyond the smell of fear and filth was a delicate feminine scent that made my nostrils flare and an aggravated huff of breath escape.

She smelled... wonderful.

I closed my eyes for a moment, picturing her yellow hair across my fingers or perhaps draped across my chest and shoulders as she curled next to me in my embrace, thankful I had rescued her.

Or her hair gripped in my fist as I fucked her.

No.

I snorted in my frustration. Those thoughts and urges were remnants of a being I no longer was. Just because I was created for breeding didn't mean I was a complete animal.

Although, when I caught her scent in the wind, it was the first time those parts of my being had been stirred in many years.

Rage began to filter through my veins because thinking of my creators, the Ghaal, reminded me of what they'd done to me, trying to set an example. I was what they had made me in more ways than one. Violence for violence, I learned from how they treated me, eventually turning my rage back on them.

Snarling, I stood and adjusted so the unit's base rested between my shoulder blades. With a heave, I lifted, holding my arms up and keeping the unit as steady as possible to move it away from the lava pits that were a threat to the female.

She screamed and started moving about, and this set me off balance.

"Stay still!" I growled out, forgetting she wouldn't be able to understand me. Where there had been confused mumbling and squealing in the unit before, there was now silence, and as I carried her down the mountain, I looked up to see her poking her head out of the unit. She screamed again when she saw me and scrambled around inside the pod, once again throwing me off balance.

With a frustrated cry, I lowered the pod to the ground, and when I straightened, the female was climbing haphazardly out of the unit. She threw me a terrified look and tried to finish exiting the pod, squeaking with terror when her clothes snagged and caught on something inside. In her desperation to get away from me, the fabric ripped, exposing her slender leg, and with another snarl, I reached out and grabbed her arm. She needed to get to safety, then we could communicate, and she would understand she was safest when she was with me.

But she fought me, slapping her hand against where I held her upper arm and screaming. When I maneuvered her so I held both her hands in one of mine, she continued to scream and struggle. I couldn't help the slight curve of my lip in amusement.

She was a fighter. *I liked that and decided we would get along.*

Almost as soon as I'd had the thought, she stopped struggling, instead looking at me with terrified eyes that filled with tears, talking to me in a soft voice with words I couldn't understand, unfamiliar syllables rolling off her tongue. Whether she was pleading for her life or trying to reason with me, I couldn't tell. Frowning, I lost my patience and hauled her up and over my shoulder, ignoring the way she beat at my back with her fists, and I carried her to the cave I called home.

Although the female stopped fighting for a time and instead slumped over my shoulder and wept, her beating on my back started anew and was joined by kicking against my abdomen when I brought her into my cave. Lowering her to the cave floor, she immediately tried to run past me toward the exit, and I snarled at her, baring my teeth and leaning forward until she cowered against the rear wall. I didn't want to frighten her further, but until we could communicate, short of tying her up, it was the only way I could get her to stay, which would go nowhere toward gaining trust.

I had a large animal skin cover which I pulled over the cave's entrance and held it in place with boulders I'm certain the small female wouldn't be able to shift. She watched me as I worked, and the expression on her soft, rounded face switched between anger and anguish. I liked her small bursts of rage—her brow would furrow, and she'd glare at me as if such a tiny female could be a threat to me.

When the cover was in front of the exit, I crouched near it across from her. Her expression shifted again, but it wasn't fear or anger this time—

it looked almost like curiosity.

Good, that's a good start.

I could work with curiosity, but fear was more difficult to overcome. As I stood, she squeaked in terror again and tried to move farther away, but with nowhere to go and her back already against the cave's rear wall, her bare heels simply scuffed against the ground.

Okay, so not curious enough to overcome her fear.

This may take some time.

CHAPTER 4

SAMARA

Had I been kidnapped or rescued? I couldn't be sure.

I'd been trying to gather my thoughts in the escape pod and maybe even enjoyed a moment of quiet when I wasn't surrounded by strange aliens on a ship and simply let the breeze cool my stress away a bit. Then I'd heard a growl or a snarl or *something,* and when I went to look, the pod had been lifted, and I was being carried across the mountains. There was no remaining calm at that point, and when I screamed too much, the creature shouted at me, a strange language full of clicks and sounds I didn't understand.

Of course, I didn't understand. I was on an *alien planet.*

My hands trembled as I gripped the pod to look over the edge, and when the creature glanced up at me, the pod balanced on his shoulders, I screamed again. His skin was a deep gun-barrel gray, practically black, dappled with angry reds and oranges like the lava against the side of the mountain. He could almost be *made* of the mountain if I didn't know better. Like the grays of his skin were cracked stone, opening to reveal lines of lava beneath.

But did I know better? This was an alien planet. What if the rocks came to life here? What if every bush and tree I thought was simply part of the landscape was a hungry creature, alive and able to come after me?

Panic set in, and when the creature placed the pod down, on instinct, I tried to run, but my stupid clothes got caught on the edges of the seat, and it held me up long enough for it to grab me.

Him, for *him,* to grab me.

Dear Lord, the man was wearing only a loincloth that barely covered anything, and I looked away as a flush crawled up my skin. His grip on my arm increased, and he started dragging me toward him, ripping my clothes further. I didn't know what else to do but scream and try to fight him off.

But this alien creature, this male, was over seven feet tall, and his chest was wider than two of me. He was a monster, and I had no chance. The fight I had burning within me tapered off as I was thrown over his shoulder. I slumped against my captor and tried not to cry too loudly.

He'd grabbed me with such ferocity it was hard to believe he was rescuing me with pure intentions. Even if we didn't understand each other, he could have waved—*do aliens wave?*—or at least tried to talk to me—maybe offered me some food or water. There were any number of ways he could have broken the ice or at least shown that he was trying to help. But the way he simply lifted the pod and carried me down the side of the mountain before grabbing and throwing me over his shoulder, it felt like I was cargo again.

Okay, Samara, think positive.

He's an alien.

Maybe he's... *shy?*

I sobbed again, almost breaking into a watery laugh as the thought formed. There was nothing I could do but wait until we got to wherever he was taking me and then assess the situation.

I didn't have to wait long, and we moved into a large cave, large enough for him to stand comfortably and for me not to hit my head even if I were sitting on his shoulders. I could only see one entrance , and therefore, only one exit. Instinct took over, and I tried to run the second my feet touched the cave's floor.

But the creature *roared* at me, exposing sharp teeth and a black tongue. His bright green eyes blazed, and he towered over me. His every attempt at intimidation absolutely *worked.*

So, I retreated toward the rear of the cave, huddled my arms around my legs again, and could only watch as he secured the only exit.

The cave was quiet as the creature and I looked at each other for what seemed like an eternity.

I knew I should at least *try* to talk to him, but *he'd* brought *me* here. Was it too much to ask that he be the first to speak? Or was the way he roared at me, him speaking to me? I shuddered at the thought. He was terrifying at that moment, and it was hard to forget as he crouched on the opposite side of the cave and watched me with his head tilted slightly like a curious puppy.

The only words he'd spoken to me were roars and shouts, and I prayed he could talk at a normal volume, even if I didn't understand what he was saying. He was terrifying to look at, and I'm not sure

I'd be able to keep my fear in check if every sound he made was at a volume that made my legs tremble with terror.

The longer he sat there watching me, the more my discomfort ebbed and made way for curiosity. I watched him back and tried to think rationally.

He hadn't attacked or tied me up. These were good signs.

Think, Samara, think.

So, he grabbed me and took me here in a hurry, but once we got here, he'd barely moved. Like he was waiting for me to make the first move. Maybe his hurry was because there was something dangerous outside? Something I didn't know about. Maybe he knew where I had come from and why I was here? That might be too much to ask. But could it be this giant, and let's be honest, slightly demonic-looking alien, was only trying to keep me safe?

Licking my lips again, I glanced around the cave. This appeared to be his home. There was a bundle of what looked like animal skin—it could almost be from a bear or buffalo-like creature, except it was a deep teal—against one wall, and a black, ashy spot near the center of the cave I assume was for fire.

God, I was thirsty.

I looked at the alien again, and he was still watching me. Blazing eyes so bright green they looked out of place with the rest of him. It was no wonder I hadn't seen him approach the pod—he was the same color as the mountains around us. *Camouflage.* It's fascinating, but there would be time to be interested in the evolutionary details of this planet later.

I hoped, at least.

Another glance around the cave and my brows furrowed. There didn't seem to be signs of more than one alien. This one had closed off the exit from the inside. Did he live alone? Were there others?

My head almost spun with the number of questions I had. I forced myself to focus, repeating what was apparently my mantra here.

Think, Samara, think.

Thirsty. I was thirsty. Life on this planet meant water, surely. I needed a drink. It was as good of a time as any to try and communicate.

"Um..." I started, and the alien's back straightened immediately, his posture alert and eyes piercing into mine. He leaned forward on his knuckles but otherwise didn't come closer, and my mouth suddenly felt drier than it had a moment ago. His stance was predatory.

"Um, may I have some water, please?" He frowned at me. Too many words. Okay. I tried again. "Water?" When he still didn't move, I rubbed my throat, then mimicked drinking. "Water? Drink?"

Abruptly, he stood, and I curled into the corner when he approached me, his sheer size enough to draw a whimper from my lips even as I attempted to keep my panic at bay and tried to remind myself he hadn't yet given me a solid reason to fear him. But as he came closer, he grabbed an animal skin bag of some sort and held it out to me. I wanted to take it, I really did, but when he was this close, the fear was all I could feel, and my limbs froze in place. He was too big and simply too intimidating for me to relax around.

With an angry huff of air through his nostrils, the alien dropped the bag at my feet and moved away to crouch once again on the opposite side of the cave.

Tentatively, I picked up the bag, and it sloshed around in my fingers. Desperation took away any second-guessing I otherwise would have done at drinking something from a stranger, and I guzzled down the water even though it was warm and tasted like minerals from a rocky stream.

His eyes widened when I finally lowered the water bag, wiping my mouth with the back of my hand. I realized too late I'd finished almost all his water, and alarm gripped my heart in a vice as I curled the near-empty bag in my fingers.

"Oh, I'm sorry! I was really thirsty. I didn't mean to drink it all."

What if water was hard to come by here, and I'd just drank his entire day's supply?

But he seemed unconcerned and didn't react when I placed the empty water bag on the floor between us. His bright green eyes bore into mine, and I tried not to blink. But every now and then, his gaze would wander, dragging down my body and lingering—on my legs, my chest, my stomach—before he would look back at my face. His gaze brought heat to my cheeks, and I wanted to look away but stayed staring at him determinedly for what felt like almost half an hour. I needed him to feel comfortable until I figured out what he wanted with me.

He stood, and I was unsuccessful in hiding my reaction as I pushed further against the cave wall. When he approached, he reached out to me, and automatically, I slapped his hand away. He withdrew his hand, looked at me quizzically, then indicated his head, then mine, and reached out to me again. Once more, I slapped his hand away, not yet ready to have him touch me. This time, he snarled, his lip curling and revealing sharp teeth and dark gums, and I shrunk under his stare.

Okay, maybe I needed to keep him busy if he was thinking about touching me.

"Food?" I said, patting my stomach. "Do you have any food? I'm hungry."

He stared at me for a moment longer before grunting and turning abruptly, moving the barrier only long enough for him to step outside. There was a shuffling and grinding of rock on rock from beyond the cave entrance before the sound of his footsteps subsided. Taking my opportunity, I hastily stood and jogged to the entrance, and exit, of the cave. Running my fingers around the edge of the animal skin, when I found a grip, I couldn't shift it. The rocks he left in the way were bigger than me, and even when I threw my entire weight against it, I couldn't get it to budge an inch.

Huffing, I returned to where I sat before, glancing around the cave for anything I could use to defend myself. I didn't want to hurt the alien creature unless I had to, but his motives still weren't clear, and I needed to be ready. A pile of bones was stacked against one of the walls, and with a shudder, I crawled toward them, finding one that looked big enough to do some damage but not so big as to hinder me if I tried to swing it. Then I grabbed one of the skins from the pile where it looked like he slept and returned to my spot at the rear of the cave, draping the animal skin over my legs and tucking the bone out of sight.

Then, I waited.

The alien returned to the cave with a dead animal of some sort slung over his shoulder. It looked like a little goat—white, gray, fluffy, and almost cute if it weren't for the six sharp horns on its little head and the tiny hooves. Four legs, but each hoof had six points on it, each looking equally as sharp and dangerous as the next.

With a grunt, my captor dropped the small

animal on the cave's floor and began to build a fire. He looked at me again as if waiting for me to do or say anything, then mumbled something in that strange language of his before returning to his task and preparing the meat. It was comforting to hear him talk at a level that wasn't a roar or shout, and my shoulders sagged slightly as I relaxed a little.

"Thank you," I whispered. His hands stopped midcut of the meat, and his gaze jerked toward me. "Um, my name is Samara. Do you have a name?" When he continued to stare at me, his eyes taking in the blanket I had over my lap before coming back to look at my face, I pointed at my chest. "Samara," I repeated, then pointed at him and raised my eyebrows.

His gaze lingered where I had pointed to my chest, and I subconsciously drew my tank top together, hiding my cleavage, however small it may be.

"Sam-ar-ah." I tried again, then pointed to him.

"Lanir," he grunted.

That must be his name, right? It sounded like *lan-ear,* but there was a weird clicking inflection on the first syllable I don't think I could replicate. So I repeated it the best I could. "Lanir. Hello." Then I waved.

His eyes narrowed, and he nodded. "S'mara."

He blended the S and the M together, but I didn't mind. So, Lanir, this demon-looking mountain alien, was intelligent enough to talk to me. That's good. If we could communicate, then maybe he could help me find the other girls. Maybe he could even lead me to other lifeforms on this planet who had the technology to take us home. Hope swelled in my chest at the possibilities as I watched Lanir cook the meat, prodding it with the end of a sharp bone. Lanir appeared mostly humanoid if I ignored the color and texture of his skin, the sharp features of his face, and his sheer size. He had one less finger than me on each hand and the same with his toes. But his large feet curled against the cave floor, and I wondered how flexible he was. Maybe his ancestors used to live in trees, or he uses his big feet to easily move about the mountains, gripping the oddly-shaped rocks.

Here I was again thinking of things I couldn't possibly get answers to, but I let my thoughts wander. It was nice to be having these thoughts. It made me relax a bit more. I'd rather wonder about all the things I could learn about this planet, a place perhaps no other humans would ever see than sit here and wallow in my fear.

When my gaze dropped to look at Lanir's feet as he crouched, I caught another glimpse of his substantial manhood, not completely covered by the loincloth. I squeaked and turned away, knowing my cheeks were burning red again. As I looked back, Lanir was watching me, his teeth slightly bared in a sneer or a snarl, I couldn't tell.

I wasn't completely innocent. I'd seen and even touched a cock before, but my lack of experience was part of the reason Dylan and I broke up, I think, although I doubted he would've admitted it to me. I'd given him a hand job, and we'd kissed, and that was about the extent of it. I'd seen dirty movies and felt so inadequate—all those women seemed to know exactly what they were doing, and I had no idea. I didn't realize until I got to college just how sheltered my life had been, and the idea of sex made me uncomfortable. The longer I waited, the more awkward I became until I dissolved into a nervous mess the moment a guy started taking off his shirt. I was only nineteen. It wasn't old by a long shot, but all other girls my age seemed to be doing things I had never even heard of, and now I'd built it up so much in my mind I didn't know where to start.

The way Lanir looked at me with that wandering gaze made me flush and think of all the things I hadn't done. To keep myself sane, I decided that Lanir was a gentle giant. He was simply a monster who only wanted companionship and understanding. While he looked like a demon, I bet, given the chance, he'd be all caresses and soft kisses when it came to lovemaking.

Scoffing, I resisted the urge to slap myself straight. Why was I even *thinking* about sex at a time like this? I shouldn't be looking at an alien who'd kidnapped me with anything other than idle curiosity and weariness. But before the smell of smoke had taken over the cave, coupled with the enticing scent of meat cooking, Lanir's scent had washed over me.

And he smelled amazing.

I expected him to smell like dirt and ash, like the mountain he lived on, but the scent was all things masculine, and I couldn't even begin to compare it to anything. But it made me tingle in all the right places and think things I shouldn't.

Looking up when there was a rumble-like growl through Lanir's chest, I startled a bit to find him standing so close to me, not having heard him approach. He bent to offer me a leg of meat, and tentatively, I accepted, taking a cautious sniff. Lanir huffed out his impatience, and when I bit down on the meat, he watched me intently. He did that a lot, huffing out through his nose angrily like a bull.

Then he reached out to touch me again, brushing my hair with his fingers.

"No," I said with as much force as I could muster as the seven-foot mountain alien man stood over me. Sitting, I came up to just above his knees, and it was difficult to maintain any kind of authority. "No touching."

Again, he withdrew his hand, and I sighed heavily, thankful he had boundaries, even if he didn't understand me.

LANIR

S'mara wouldn't let me touch her.

How was I supposed to join our minds and learn her language if she wouldn't let me touch her? It wouldn't take long. I could connect to her mind through a practiced touch and learn, and then we could talk. I huffed out through my nose again, stalked away, crouched on the opposite side of the fire and ripped a leg of the gorae, throwing the whole thing in my mouth and crunching down on the bones. I resumed watching her. She was weary of me—this was to be expected—but she didn't seem afraid except for when I got too close or tried to touch her.

I didn't want to have to force contact. I didn't want to force her to do anything, not after the way I'd been treated by the Ghaal. But S'mara needed to know the danger she was in and that she was safer with me.

How could I explain it to her without her language?

I watched S'mara eat and offered her another water bag. She sipped between mouthfuls, keeping an eye on me and looking weary every time I moved or shifted in any way.

"I need to talk to you," I grunted out, knowing she couldn't understand me, but frustration was getting the better of me, and I needed to feel like I was trying. "I need to touch you to do that."

She tilted her head at me and put down the leftover bone. I wondered why she didn't eat that too, but then studying what I could see of her tiny teeth, maybe she couldn't.

Then she spoke. "Ne-eed."

I jolted, staring at her. She was mimicking my language, picking the word I had repeated. Her pronunciation was off, the same way I couldn't repeat her name back to her the way she said it. Her small pink lips lifted into a tentative smile at my reaction, and I returned the expression only for her to look slightly alarmed.

My smile dropped, and I frowned at her. Surely, she could see I was trying not to frighten her.

"Need," I repeated.

"Ne-eed." I decided it was as close as she was going to get. But how do I explain to her what that word meant? I was no good at this, somewhat wishing my brother, Ilk, or even Sahcor was here. Ilk was more levelheaded, always in command, and Sahcor could be a bit of a loner, but he was a good problem-solver.

But when I imagined either one of them here, trying to talk to S'mara, a bolt of jealousy stabbed through my gut. I didn't want *anyone* near her. The possessiveness surprised me, and I tried to keep the snarl from my face. S'mara was mine to protect and care for, to keep safe, and teach her about our planet. I didn't need anyone's help. In time, she would trust and not fear me as she does now. I'd figure it out with her.

I pointed to my mouth. "Talk."

S'mara leaned forward slightly, smiling now. "Taulk."

"Close enough," I grumbled, and she smiled wider. She was odd but not unattractive. S'mara was petite and fragile but with wide hips and large thighs. I wanted to grab them and taste her sweet cunt on my tongue, and I shuddered at the thought. When I gazed back at S'mara, she was staring wide-eyed at my crotch, and I realized my arousal was on display to her. Grunting again, I readjusted. I wouldn't force her. She needed to feel safe with me. Her eyes traveled to my face slowly, and when she met my gaze, her cheeks flushed pink, and she turned away.

Did she feel the attraction too? Simply her being near to me triggered parts of my instinct I hadn't even thought about in years. She looked like me... *almost*. A smaller, more fragile, delicate, feminine version of me, and it was difficult not to picture what it would be like to have her tiny frame under my body and what her face would look like in the throes of pleasure as I pierced her with my cock. As I watched her, S'mara's eyelids fluttered, and she blushed again. My distracting thoughts would be causing my pheromones to pulse through me and release into the air.

Aphrodisiacs. Not drugs. They wouldn't make her do anything she didn't already want to do, but they would stir up any existing arousal.

S'mara fidgeted where she sat, and my eyes widened.

She *was* attracted to me. She was thinking about fucking too. Surely, she was not also designed for breeding? Not in the same sense I was. I'm certain she was a biologically organic organism, not created in a lab. Did her planet have genetic engineering? Is that why her hips and thighs were so lush and plentiful compared to the pinch of her waist? To bear many offspring?

Snarling, I threw the bone I'd been holding against the cave wall in frustration. I needed to concentrate. The move made S'mara squeak again the way she does when frightened, and this only enraged me more. Now she was scared again.

Curling my hands into fists, I rubbed them against my eyes. I needed to focus.

When I looked back at S'mara, she watched me with curiosity again. She mumbled something in her strange language, and the syllables rolled off her tongue rather than the sharp, clipped tone of mine. "Ewtyred?" I think she was asking me a question. I stared at her, and she placed her palms together, pressing the back of one of her hands against her cheek and tilting her head. "Schleep?" She closed her eyes for a moment and made small snoring noises.

I barked out a laugh, and she jumped again before smiling herself.

Less fear. Time to talk again.

"Talk," I said again, keeping my words short. "Lanir, S'mara, need talk." I added hand gestures, but wasn't sure she understood. She frowned, and I repeated. The female again attempted to repeat my words, her small pink tongue darting out between her lips at odd intervals. The attempt was appalling, but she was trying, and that filled me with a bit of hope.

My patience didn't last as long as I'd like, and I stood, moving toward the other end of the cave. With a yelp, she stood as well, her eyes darting between my outstretched hands and the arousal I couldn't hide under my loincloth, my cock hard and ready for her.

"Itheenkeyneedtewgotewthhbaathroum." She threw a lot of syllables at me, and I paused, lowering my hand and angry at how she breathed a sigh of relief when I once again stopped my attempts to touch her.

When I halted in my approach, she flushed again, pointing to her cunt. My arousal swelled, and once again, her eyelids became heavy as my pheromones permeated the space between us, and she rubbed her thighs together. Did she want to have sex? If she were willing, I'd be happy to oblige. My cock twitched, and I grumbled out a barely contained moan. We didn't need to talk to have sex, and I glanced at my cock as it twitched under my loincloth.

With another squeak, she shook her head rapidly from side to side and cupped her hands in front of her cunt, as if trying to shield me from the scent of her arousal. "Baathroum." She touched her belly, then pointed to the empty water bag.

Oh. I knew what she needed.

With another grunt, I turned and moved toward the cave's entrance, looking back to check she was following. Heaving the rocks out of the way, I pulled at the cover and stepped outside, staring at the sun as it neared the horizon. S'mara tentatively emerged from the cave, and I pointed at the ground. "Empty your bladder here."

She looked startled, then glanced around before back at me, hugging her arms around herself. Did she need to relieve herself or not? Pointing at the ground again, I then jabbed a finger at her. "Relieve yourself." My words ended with a snarl, and she jumped slightly.

This would be much easier if she would let me learn her language.

S'mara shook her head, lifted her hand, made a swirling motion with her finger, and then pointed at me.

She didn't want me to look.

Narrowing my eyes at her, I slowly turned around, my senses on high alert to make sure she didn't try to flee. There was a shuffling before I heard the stream of urine hitting rock and a satisfied sigh. After a moment, I sensed her stand and turned to face her.

She took one look at me, glanced at my cock before resting her gaze on my eyes, and bolted.

With a roar, I took chase, using my arms as much as my legs to leap between and over the rocky face of the mountainside. We were not out of the area where lava was a danger, not to mention the ever-present threat of the Ghaal. She didn't understand the danger she was in, but she wouldn't let me communicate with her either.

I caught up with her quickly, scooped her up in my arms as I ran past, keeping my speed up, and turned back toward the cave. She struggled for a brief period, but she had given up by the time I had reached the cave's entrance. I placed S'mara gently on her feet, she padded softly toward the back of the cave, laid down, grabbed some fur, and rolled it over herself before she turned to face the wall.

"I'm trying to protect you," I muttered after I had closed off the cave again.

She huffed out a small breath but said nothing, and eventually fell asleep without another word.

CHAPTER 6

SAMARA

When I woke, my mountain alien keeper was still there. The sunlight streamed in through a small gap at the top of the cave's entrance, the fire having long gone out, but the smell of smoke lingered in the small space.

Lanir was leaning against the wall near the exit with his legs stretched out elegantly in front of him. He'd both frightened and impressed me last night, moving with speed and agility I wouldn't have thought possible for someone his size. It seemed as much as he looked like the environment here, he was practically a part of it. As he ran back toward the cave, carrying me protectively in his arms, he shifted and vaulted over and around the boulders and lava pits with barely a glance.

I sat and cried out as a sharp pain hit my stomach. Unfolding the blanket, I rolled up my tank top and hissed as the fabric shifted over my belly button. Shit, it looked like it was getting infected. The wound around where my piercing had been partially ripped out was angry and red, with congealed pus and blood surrounding the surgical steel of the piercing. Shit, shit, *shit.* What do I do? Do I take the piercing out? It seemed a good idea, I didn't want the wound to heal over it.

But I also couldn't wash my hands.

As gently as I could manage, I untwisted one end of the piercing, biting my bottom lip in an attempt to cover my whimpers. I tugged slightly on the bar, and it didn't budge. With a deep breath, I pulled harder and couldn't contain my cry when I pulled it free, blood and pus oozing fresh from the wound. Bunching up my tank, I dabbed gently at my stomach, whimpering and sobbing as the pain came back with a new intensity.

There was a snarl above me.

Slowly, I looked up. Lanir loomed over me, his sharp teeth bared threateningly and his lip rippling as his snarl continued. He wasn't looking at my face but where I clutched my top against my bleeding stomach. He barked something at me, but I shook my head. I didn't understand what he wanted. With another deep growl, he crouched in front of me and wrestled my hands away from my stomach. I fought him, not wanting him to see the blood, unsure how he'd react.

Lanir maneuvered my hands until he clasped my wrists in one of his hands and pressed them against the cave's wall above where I sat. With surprising gentleness, he lifted my top, hissing out a breath through his teeth when I whimpered in pain. He stared at the wound for a long time, then abruptly dropped my hands from his grip, bounded toward the cave's entrance, and left, replacing the cover behind him.

Okay…

I didn't know what to think of this, so I simply waited. When he didn't return immediately, I reached out for the water bag and drank whatever meager rations were left, hoping this wouldn't anger him. I didn't want to be selfish, but I was thirsty and hungry, and since he'd gone to the trouble of hunting for me, it would feel ungrateful to ask to be fed again so soon.

I was angry last night but mostly at myself. Left alone with my thoughts, I couldn't even explain why I ran after he took me to go to the bathroom. It wasn't like he'd tried to hurt me. But again, I was captive, and no matter how nice he was to me, I was still essentially in a cage with no idea as to his motives or what he planned to do. The constant reminder of his arousal sparked panic in me, and since I couldn't be sure what he was thinking of planning, my wandering thoughts got the better of me. I'd given up trying to struggle after he grabbed me, realizing I would need to play this through and see where it took me.

I still didn't know if there were more of Lanir's kind. What would happen when they got back? Was I dinner? I had no way of knowing.

No, that wasn't it. He wasn't going to eat me. Lanir was looking after me, but why? Lanir owed me nothing—he'd simply found me. Maybe I was the equivalent of a stray puppy on this planet in need of looking after. I thought about how he kept reaching out to stroke my hair. Maybe it was an affectionate thing.

Maybe I was being too hard on the big guy. I needed to remember that he hadn't—yet—tried to harm me, and I still had a weapon stowed away just in case he tried.

It's time to try to clear my mind again because for a moment there yesterday, I thought we made some progress communicating with each other. I'll admit my usual positivity had been hard to maintain at one hundred percent because, well, obviously, this isn't a normal sort of situation. But I'm alive, I'm fed, and there's someone here who at least seems to be trying to help me.

I hissed through my teeth again when moving reignited pain in my belly button, and I was about to see if I could find some more water to pour over the wound when Lanir came back. He turned to me, and I tried my best not to cower under his glare, a deep frown etched on his face and a snarl to match. I smiled at him, and he halted in his steps for a moment, seemingly confused. Apparently, he decided I was trying to trick him and frowned at me again.

He pulled out an animal skin bag and moved toward me, emptying the contents on to the cave's floor by my legs. He had two fresh water bags and a handful of strange-looking plants. Lanir reached for my top, and on instinct, I slapped his hand away, cursing myself immediately and gritting my teeth against doing it again when he reached out again, holding my eye contact the entire time. This time, I didn't stop him and allowed him to roll up the fabric, his fingers grazing against the sensitive skin of my waist, making me shudder.

I yelped as he grabbed my thighs and yanked me down so I was lying on my back. When I went to move, he snarled and placed his palm on my chest, holding me down. His hand took up almost my entire chest, and for a reason I couldn't begin to comprehend, it felt like a strangely erotic move. I shuddered again, a sharp intake of breath brushing past my lips as we locked eyes.

He still smelled amazing, and I breathed it in, trying to relax.

I told myself *he was only trying to help*, even though I had no way to be sure.

Lanir's lip twitched as if he were going to snarl again, but I lifted my hands and grabbed his wrist, hoping he would ease up just a bit on the pressure against my rib cage. His skin was smooth but oddly textured, like a stone benchtop in an expensive kitchen. He released me and guided my hands to hold my top up. He held up the plants one by one and spoke to me, pointing to my belly button. I had no idea what he was saying, but I couldn't keep my eyes off his face. There was something different when he talked this way like the animal was gone and an intelligent being was there. It was so strange. He could pick me up like I was nothing, but he was oddly gentle with me.

I guess, as I always do, I should hope for the best.

It seemed Lanir was going to treat my wound, and I gritted my teeth in anticipation of the pain. First, he popped some clear, round, berry-looking things between his fingers, releasing the oil into his palm. He splashed some water on my belly, and I hissed, then cried out when he rubbed the oil into my stomach. It stung like soap, and while I assumed Lanir knew what he was doing, it was impossible to override the part of my mind that wanted to escape the pain. He snarled when I tried to wiggle away and used more water to wash away the oil.

Tears sprung in my eyes, and he looked at me again, lifting his lip and exposing his sharp teeth.

"I'm sorry," I whispered, shrinking away from his glare. "It hurts. I'm trying to be still, Lanir."

His shoulders visibly relaxed when I spoke his name, but I tensed again when he picked up the next plant. It looked like a weed, deep green with dark purple veins through the large leaves and a long, thin stalk going down to gray roots, still covered in soil. Lanir stripped the leaves, crushed them between his palms, and ground them into a paste.

Our eyes met as he moved again, and his expression changed.

Almost like he was apologizing for what he had to do.

My breath caught in my throat. It was such a sweet look of longing and apology and so... *human.* Steeling myself, I nodded and squeezed my eyes shut. When the plant goop hit my stomach, the pain was instant and searing, and I cried out. Lanir shifted quickly, straddling me and clamping my legs between his thighs and holding my wrists so I couldn't move the plant from my stomach. I wanted to lie there and accept he was trying to help, but my body twisted, and I pulled at his grip, desperate to get the plant away from my skin and stop the stinging pain.

I opened my eyes, shining with tears I tried to blink away and held Lanir's gaze. He looked in pain himself as if my pain was hurting him. I hiccupped slightly and bit my lip, trying to bear through it.

Then, almost as quickly as it started, the pain was gone.

Startled, I looked down. The goop was still over the wound, but now it felt almost numb. Was it healing? Or had the plant just numbed it? I glanced at Lanir again, and he brushed the inside of my wrist with his thumb.

No longer distracted by pain, I couldn't help taking in the lines of his arms and chest leading down to a well-defined six-pack and... oh...

Lanir was aroused again.

Flushing, I looked away from his erection that strained against the cloth covering his crotch and back at his face. His eyelids were heavy with need, and his lips were slightly parted, his chest heaving with each breath. I shuddered under the intensity of his gaze and felt my arousal spike. Lanir grunted a few words, and I slowly shook my head without removing my gaze from his.

"I don't understand," I whispered. Feeling bold and horny for reasons I couldn't pin down, I moved my hand. Lanir released my forearm, and I reached up to stroke his cheek. His skin was so strange but not uncomfortable to touch. I kind of liked it and traced my fingers up and down his arm, touching, exploring, and familiarizing myself with this being, making a connection when we had no words to use. Lanir released another puff of air through his nostrils, like a bull again, and I smiled, unable to help my amusement. How could he be intelligent enough to care for a wound but still animal enough he moved and grunted like one?

And where was his family?

Was he alone out here?

The idea clenched my heart in grief for him. If that were the case, then Lanir taking and looking after me would not be so strange. Maybe he was simply lonely and looking for some company. What happened to his family? Were they dead? Did they leave him alone? I wanted the answers, and the more I searched his eyes, the more I desperately wanted to know about him.

If only we could talk.

With a thud, I jumped as Lanir dropped onto his elbows, lying on top of me but careful not to touch my stomach. His face was inches from mine, and his eyes were blazing. God, why was I so turned on by him? Shifting his weight, he ran a finger gently along my lower lip, and I trembled.

"Lanir…" I didn't know if I would ask him to stop or to keep going. A sense of reckless abandon was filling me. I was lost on an alien planet, so what's to stop me from doing whatever I wanted? Who knows, I could die tomorrow. All I could think of right now was it was taking all of my willpower not to cant my hips and rub against Lanir, inviting him to touch me more.

But part of me was still weary of him.

Lanir had paused when I said his name, and when I didn't speak further, he cupped my face, his warm palm encompassing my cheek. I panicked when he snaked his hands up, tangled his fingers in my hair and pressed against my scalp.

His hand was practically as big as my head—he could snap my neck without a second thought.

"No, no, I can't do this." I shoved hard at his chest, and he looked down at the movement. He snarled at me, and my panic spiked. "Lanir, let me go. Let me *go.*" When I slapped at his chest, pushing and grunting to get him off me, his gaze was thunderous, and it was only my desperate need for space that kept me from shrinking under his gaze.

Lanir lifted himself off me and retreated to the other side of the cave once more.

7

LANIR

So close. I had been *so close* to touching her mind and learning her language.

Seconds, I would only need seconds to get enough to explain to her what I was doing. Then it would depend on the complexity of her language, but I could learn most languages in a few minutes at most—longer if I wanted to pick up all physical gestures and body language as well as slang and nicknames if the culture had any.

So. Close.

If I had moved faster, we would have been

talking by now.

But I was so distracted by her.

My cock ached against my meager clothing—even the strip of thin leather around my hips felt like too much. The only thing I wanted touching me was S'mara. I hadn't felt like this in... I couldn't remember when. What the Ghaal had done to me to try and get me to breed had only increased my rage and made me press down harder on the instincts they had designed me to have. I couldn't control my pheromones, though, and S'mara looked at me as if she *wanted* me to touch her, and that only made it harder.

Because she was so soft and fragile, and when I foolishly touched her lip, I almost couldn't stop myself when she started panicking and pushing me away. The animalistic part of me *begged* my mind to let go of the control I clung to so I could simply take her, hold her down, and fuck her.

But I wouldn't take her against her will.

Not now, not ever.

No matter the physical discomfort it caused me or how much I needed to concentrate my anger to keep myself under control, I wouldn't make S'mara afraid of me.

At least not any more than she already was.

Glancing at her across the cave, she was tapping tentatively against the herbs I had packed against her wound, now dried and hardened. When she started to pick at the corner with her fingers, I snarled at her. "Leave it… it will heal your wound."

My snarl, more than my words, resulted in her withdrawing her hand, and she pouted at me.

I needed to gain her trust. Treating her wound would have been a good step, but then I had pinned her to the ground and touched her. Baring my teeth at my stupidity, I stood, glancing at S'mara as she watched me wearily.

"Let's go hunting. I'll teach you what to eat." Later, I'd teach her some words, but I was too frustrated to have the patience for it right now. Maybe if I took her outside and showed her some things, she would begin to trust me enough to let me touch her mind.

S'mara sat, and I growled low and deep, cutting off the sound when her eyes widened.

"Get up," I said, indicating she should stand. I then pointed to my spear. "Hunting."

"Hunting," she repeated, not even close to the correct pronunciation but close enough. I pointed again to the spear, then to me, then to her, then to the cave's exit. She seemed to understand and nodded enthusiastically, rewarding me with a smile. Before I removed the screen in front of the door, I halted—maybe she'd feel safer if she had a weapon.

Grabbing a bone blade, I shoved it toward her, holding the blunt end out for her to grab. She did it very slowly and turned the blade in her hands a few times before giving me an uncertain look.

"Hunt," I said.

"Hunt," she repeated.

I led her out of the cave.

Finding a herd of gorae shouldn't be too much trouble, and they were small enough S'mara would be able to finish the kill with the blade if my spear wasn't a clean kill. Leading her down the side of the mountain, I avoided the areas with the most lava pits and made sure to point out all the ones along the way so she knew to avoid them. S'mara already seemed aware of the danger of the lava, so perhaps she also had it on her home planet.

When she stumbled on the rocks, I held my hand out to steady her. She took it gratefully, her small hand wrapping around two of my fingers as she gingerly made her way to the base of the mountain. S'mara appeared even more fragile out here against the wild. Her clothes were thin and almost rags— I'd need to make her some as well as shoes since her feet were bare. But we wouldn't be venturing far, and as long as we steered clear of the sandy soils near the woodlands, she would be safe without shoes. The eylaks lived under that soil and would shoot a sharp barb into your foot if you walked over them. The poison wasn't enough to paralyze me, only to make me woozy for a while. I'd been stung once before and made it back to the cave, then rested it off. I don't recall it being an issue, but it was uncomfortable and left me in a weakened and vulnerable state for a long while, and I don't like being weak. But the poison would be enough to take down S'mara almost instantly, then they would swarm over her and pick the flesh from her bones.

But she was safe with me.

S'mara followed me without complaint or saying anything, clutching her knife, although it looked out of place in her hands. Her eyes moved rapidly between her feet to watch where she stepped and to the landscape, taking in a planet that was alien to her. I shouldn't take for granted the situation she was in and the fact that everything about this world was strange to her, including me. When the rocks flattened out, she looked at her feet less and less and spent more time gazing around her, taking in the plant life.

I chuckled when she jumped slightly as a chipra came swooping down near her head. The tiny flying creatures were harmless and lived in large flocks in the top of the trees of the woodlands, but it was nesting season, and they were simply warning her to stay away.

When another swooped, and S'mara squealed in surprise. I laughed again, and this time, she shot me a glare, but before she turned away, I saw the slight hint of a smile on her lips.

Progress.

The gorae weren't far from the base of the mountain, and I held out an arm to halt S'mara's steps. She peeked over my arm to look at our prey and let loose a strange cooing sound. I frowned at her, and S'mara grinned at me, pointing to the gorae. "Sewcewte," she whispered before holding her fingers up to her nose and made a pinching motion, "Wittlenosies."

Shrugging, I assumed she meant food and threw my spear.

The kill wasn't clean, and I snarled at myself. S'mara screamed, and the other gorae fled at the sound. I growled at her. "I know it wasn't a clean kill, but you don't need to make such a big deal about it."

I never wanted creatures to be in pain, even those I needed for food. A clean kill was a good kill, but in my haste to feed S'mara, my aim had been off, and the spear had gone through the gorae's shoulder and chest rather than through the throat. Grabbing S'mara's arm, I dragged her toward the pitiful bleating creature. We needed to put it out of its misery.

She stood over the animal, clutching the knife to

her chest with her lip quivering and eyes watering. My anger grew. As if I didn't feel bad enough about the creature's suffering without S'mara beginning to cry. Angrily, I pointed to the knife and then to the gorae.

S'mara looked horrified and shook her head rapidly. She dropped the knife and took a step back, mumbling gibberish at me in a high-pitched voice.

I didn't understand.

With a snarl, I snatched the knife and finished the kill. Ignoring S'mara's cry, I slung the carcass over my shoulder, grabbing S'mara when she didn't move to follow and holding her over my other shoulder before sprinting back toward the cave.

I didn't understand her reaction. I thought she would enjoy learning about the planet, and the first thing she needed to learn was how to hunt and fend for herself. Gorae were small enough that even she could carry a kill over her shoulders if she balanced it right, and they were plentiful across the island. But when faced with the opportunity to finish the kill mercifully, she'd cried and protested. She was still crying as she lay over my shoulder, her small hands pressed against my back to balance herself against the jostling of my run. She kept saying my name and then murmuring things I didn't understand, and I snarled again, frustrated once more at her refusal to let me connect my mind to hers so we could communicate.

I didn't want to force her, but there were dangers on this planet she needed to know of, and if she left me with no choice, I would have to pin her down and take her language.

The idea of pinning S'mara under me filled my mind with distracting thoughts, and suddenly, I was all too aware of the curve of her thighs under my palm and the press of her breasts against my back. She had a generous backside for her size, and with her slung over my shoulder like this, it would be so easy to touch her, to let my fingers wander up her thigh...

No.

Not unless she let me.

With a roar of frustration, I put on a burst of speed and ran the rest of the way home.

CHAPTER 8

SAMARA

When the giant alien man says you're both going out to get food, you go.

What I didn't know was that Lanir expected me to finish off the kill of a fluffy goat-like creature that looked up at me with big doe eyes, and I just folded. Lanir, as he often seems to do, responded with rage and finished the kill before scooping up both the dead animal and me and raced back to the cave. Halfway back, I'd managed to stem my tears—it was difficult to cry when you were being jostled against the rock-hard shoulder of an alien.

Besides, he was distracting me.

At first, Lanir held me around the back of my thighs, and I tried and failed to get a grip on his back as he ran, and for a moment, his fingers danced across the back of my legs and eventually between my thighs. I remained silent and as still as I could manage, but he explored no further.

After that, all I could think of was the feel of his back muscles rippling underneath my fingers as he ran. I wanted to trace the lines of them, and without thought, I started to before he snarled again and put on another burst of speed.

Lanir dropped me on the cave's floor as gently as he could manage in his rage, I supposed. It was clear I'd upset him by not finishing the kill but he'd put me on the spot. I realized now it was naïve of me to think gathering food in the wild would be anything other than hunting, considering this is how he'd fed me yesterday, but I honestly wasn't expecting him to want me to make the kill. My meat came in packets, already cut and displayed so it no longer resembled the animal it came from. Of course, we all knew, but no one wanted to think about it, and just how much I had taken for granted back home washed over me as I slumped against the rear of the cave.

Lanir closed off the entrance to the cave with more angry grunting, and I watched him under my lashes, my head ducked down to my chest.

I had a plan.

At least, I thought I did.

I wanted to earn Lanir's trust, then maybe he wouldn't watch me like a hawk and refuse to turn around now when I needed to pee. *Then I would… what? Leave? And go where?* I had no idea where the nearest civilization was or even if there *was* other life on this planet.

Another thought occurred to me, and my heart sank in sympathy.

What if Lanir was abandoned here too? Just like me? What if somewhere on this planet are friends or others like him he was kidnapped with, and he could never find them? So he lives alone.

Then I come along, and he tries to look after me. But who knows how long he's been alone, so his social etiquette may not be up to scratch. Maybe he simply wanted company, and I will admit, I'm very thankful not to be alone. Another spike of pain radiated through my chest when I thought of the other girls, and I clamped a hand over my pounding heart. God, I hope they found each other or someone to help them, or both.

I wanted to find the other girls, but I needed to be Lanir's friend first.

I needed to try harder.

With another grunt, Lanir dropped himself in front of the fire pit, and with the bone blade, he began to prepare the meat. He glanced up when I crawled closer and stopped by the edge of the fire.

"Shall I start the fire?" I whispered, hating that I didn't have more courage. When he only stared blankly at me, I pointed at the fire, then rubbed my hands together. "Fire. I can make fire?"

His chin jerked in what I hoped was a nod, and I nodded back, moving to the side of the cave to collect from the small stock of wood and twigs he kept there. They were strange and rubbery, but I'd seen Lanir burn them yesterday, so it must be possible.

I tried rubbing the sticks together like I'd seen it done in the movies, but nothing happened.

In trying to make it up to Lanir, I'd only proven, once again, how useless I was on this planet. I felt tears stinging at the back of my eyes once more and wiped my face angrily. Lanir watched me, and I met his eyes, biting my bottom lip to stop it from trembling as the feeling of uselessness threatened to overpower me. His eyes were so green and bright that it was a strange contrast to the dark, ashy color of his skin with the deep red coloring mixed in—a demon with gorgeous green eyes.

He abandoned the meat and wiped his hands on his loincloth before moving around behind me. Panicked slightly at his proximity, I whimpered when he crouched behind me, his enormous thighs on either side of my waist, and he reached around and took my hands in his.

I was trembling, and Lanir stopped moving. I could feel his eyes on me but dared not turn around. His body heat was driving every other thought from my mind. Why were we even building a fire when he was so hot?

Oh, right, food. I forgot.

My breathing increased when I couldn't think straight, and Lanir's deep voice muttered some soothing words I couldn't understand in my ear. His lips were so close to my skin as he leaned over me, encasing me with his body.

"I'm sorry," I whispered, not even entirely sure what I was apologizing for. For being afraid of him? For trembling under his touch and not being able to stop? For not finishing the kill when he asked me to?

But I wasn't afraid of him, was I? Not even with his body wrapped around mine like this. In fact, I felt safer like this than I had since the moment I'd been abducted in the first place. With a small sigh, I leaned slightly back, and Lanir's posture stiffened as I leaned against him. I held my breath, hoping I hadn't offended him, and when he began to stroke my arms again, I relaxed.

I felt like crying. The accumulation of everything that happened was piling up on me, and I could stay as positive as I wanted, but the reality of the situation was terrifying.

Thank God I had Lanir to look after me.

I sighed again and tilted my head back against his chest. Opening my eyes, his bright green ones stared down at me with an expression I couldn't read. My mouth was dry at the sight of him, and I licked my lips. Lanir groaned as his gaze was drawn to the movement, and I shuddered again. When we were like this, and I wasn't faced head-on with just how different he looked to me, it felt so… *safe*. There simply wasn't another word for it. Lanir was a large, masculine force surrounding me, protecting and keeping me safe from unknown dangers.

The urge to kiss him crept into my mind, and I watched his lips as he had mine.

It's a crazy thought, right?

But something about the way he looked at me…

Lanir snarled again, but not with the same aggression he usually showed, but more a slight ripple of his lip as a deep growl rumbled through his chest. I cleared my throat and pointed a finger at the fire, not moving my arm much as his hands were still wrapped around my wrists.

"Fire?" I croaked out, barely able to form the word through the world of impure thoughts that permeated my mind—thoughts I'd barely had about any men, let alone a giant alien.

Glancing up again to find Lanir watching me, he jerked his chin again, more a sideways motion than downward, then he shifted and slid his hands down over mine and guided me to pick up two of the smaller twigs. I still didn't understand how the rubber was meant to burn, but Lanir showed me how to twist a couple of them into a rope-like configuration and grab each end. When pulled apart rapidly, there were sparks.

I gasped and laughed out loud at the sight, and Lanir's chest rumbled in what almost sounded like a chuckle. We did it again over the thin, dry twigs, and when they caught fire, Lanir showed me how to stack the heavier wood around it to keep the blaze going. He shifted back, and I turned, kneeled, faced him, and clapped my hands together.

"I did it!" Lanir's lip lifted into almost a smirk at my elation at starting a fire, and I jabbed a finger at his chest, laughing myself. "Don't you laugh at me! That's the first time I've ever started a fire without matches."

His smirk dropped, and he looked down at my hand. Uh-oh, have I offended him again? I went to withdraw my hand, and he snatched it, bringing it back toward him and placing my palm flat against his chest. A low, rumbling growl vibrated under my fingertips, and his eyes closed. Frowning, I began to slowly stroke his chest like I was petting an animal. The rumbling increased, and when his eyes opened, and he watched me again, his lids were heavy with desire.

Did I just turn him on? I thought he just wanted to be petted.

Glancing down, his erection was once again pressing insistently against the fabric of his loincloth, and I gasped and turned my head away. Lanir's hand found my chin and turned me back to face him. He inhaled deeply, and the growling through his chest started anew.

He was so warm and so impossibly gentle. I wanted to touch his chest to feel more of the strange texture of his skin. I wanted to know what it would feel like to have him on top of me.

I mean, if I'm going to die on an alien planet, I might as well lose my virginity first, right?

Shaking my head, I tried to get rid of the thought. But now it was there, it wouldn't go away. Lanir had morphed from kidnapper to rescuer to a sexual being who was apparently thinking the same things I was.

But we couldn't communicate. What if I couldn't explain to him I was inexperienced, and he simply plunged that giant cock into me without mercy? The thought sent a shudder down my spine and drew a whimper from my lips. God, that shouldn't turn me on. Lanir growled again, this time baring his teeth at me. But his gaze was still full of desire, and I panicked when he traced his thumb along my bottom lip.

Turning, I pointed to the discarded meat. "Food. Fire. Cook." Then I rubbed my stomach. "Hungry."

Lanir's eyes followed my movement, and he

slowly withdrew his hand, offering me a sizzling look before moving away to finish preparing our meal.

LANIR

S'mara was letting me touch her, and I could have taken the chance to learn her language. But the touch was different, and how could I concentrate on learning her language when all I could think about was her small hands wrapped around my cock, guiding it into her waiting cunt.

But S'mara appeared less afraid of me with every passing moment, and now I no longer cursed the thoughts and urges that distracted me constantly. Remnants of who I was made to be, desires and needs driven into my very DNA I couldn't deny when there was a compatible female so close calling to me with the scent of her arousal—a scent that increased when I touched her.

She wanted me as I did her. My chest swelled with pride at the thought, immediately followed by a scowl at the idea of the dangers that lurked outside this cave. It wasn't safe for us to stay here, not long term—the Ghaal would have seen the pod land and no doubt knew of the cargo.

They would come after her.

We would need to leave.

I growled at myself as I prepped the meat. I should have taken the chance to learn her language, then I could have communicated with her all these things she needed to know. Glancing over at S'mara, she sat with her legs tucked underneath her by the fire, basking in its warmth. But she was watching me, not how I prepped the meat, but her gaze was traveling over my body. When she met my eyes, her cheeks flushed pink. She smiled and turned away.

My S'mara was shy.

Had she been with a male before? The idea filled me with a possessive rage, but I didn't know the culture of where she came from. Maybe females took on many mates. But S'mara seemed shy to my touch, and while her body reacted, she seemed unsure what to do.

Maybe she was to be mine and only mine.

I glanced at her again. She was so small and fragile. I wouldn't want to hurt her.

The image of her underneath me, her small hands gripping my arms as I fucked into her sweet cunt slapped across my conscious mind with such clarity I almost dropped the knife. With another snarl, I brought my thoughts back into line.

She'd be mine. Soon enough.

CHAPTER 9

SAMARA

With a stretch, I woke, my feet tangled in a bundle of fur and animal hide that I'd attempted to kick off during the night. When I raised my arms, I exhaled loudly. "Phowar."

I smelled. *Bad.*

Sitting up, I flapped my arms around a bit. Last night before bed I'd managed to wash quickly using water from one of Lanir's skin water bags and a cloth, but it wasn't enough. What I really needed was a shower or a bath, but at this stage, I'd settle for a creek. Lanir hadn't indicated the creek we collected our water from was safe to swim in, but then again, I hadn't been able to ask. He was awake already, now watching me with a twisted frown after I'd flapped my arms around. I laughed and smiled at him, and he relaxed and went back to sharpening his knife. Lanir didn't wash, at least, not that I'd seen beyond removing blood and dirt from his hands before and after prepping food. Yet he didn't smell of body odor like I did. He smelled of a musky sweetness, an earthly scent that wafted around him and seemed to get stronger when we stood close to each other.

He smelled amazing.

Inwardly, I cringed. I hoped my smell wasn't offensive to him.

Lanir had given no indication it was, no crinkling of his nose when he was near me. Just the opposite, he would inhale deeply as if I were the most incredible-smelling thing he'd ever come across. The action always sent a tingle down my spine. It was so animalistic but strangely intimate too.

Lanir didn't seem to keep a storage of food, but where would he keep it? While it wasn't obnoxiously hot on this planet, it wasn't cold either, not during the day at least, and I can't imagine meat left out would last long. So he hunted daily and had indicated last night we would go out again today. After this, repeating the word I now think means *hunt,* whereas yesterday I thought it was *food,* he watched me with concern, glancing between the knife and me. Through hand gestures, I think I had indicated to him that I would watch him hunt. Watch and learn.

Maybe eventually, I could work up the nerve to do it myself.

I didn't suppose I had much of a choice.

I'd woken up invigorated again, despite feeling sweaty, dirty, and smelly, and was ready to once again launch into life on this planet. I didn't want to linger on all the things and people I would never do or see again. I think I'd sink into a spiral of darkness and not be able to get out of it if I did. I was slowly dealing with it every new day, a fresh reminder that this was real, and there may be no going back. But I had a companion who looked after me, wanted to teach me, and with any luck, one day we'd be able to communicate with each other.

Hopefully, by the time that day came, I could explain to him there were others, and we could find them.

Standing and stretching again, I helped myself to a swig of mineral-tasting water and padded over to Lanir. He stopped sharpening the knife and watched me approach, and consciously, I tucked my hands under my arms, hoping again I didn't smell so bad it bothered him. After we'd eaten, I resolved to try to ask Lanir if I could bathe. We'd collected more water yesterday, but I imagined we would need more this afternoon.

"Can I help with anything?" I asked, fully aware he couldn't understand me but tired of living in silence. I'd opted to simply speak out loud whenever I wanted to. Lanir was grumpy and snarled a lot but never seemed offended by my rambling. I spoke at length last night about home and what I would be doing if it were an evening on Earth. He'd watched me, sitting cross-legged across the fire from me, and listened. Even though he didn't understand a word of what I was saying, it felt good to talk.

It felt more... *normal.*

I pointed to the knife, and Lanir shook his head, sliding it into his belt and standing. I had to crane my neck to look up at him, and he held my gaze before tilting his head toward the cave's entrance as if to say *ready?*

"Let's go." In return, I smiled at him and was rewarded with an odd, lopsided smile. Lanir grabbed his spear and went to work to shift the heavy rocks and animal skin out of the way. I blinked as we stepped into the sunlight, shielding my eyes from the sun with my hand and looking out over the horizon. There were birds or something swooping around as usual—the ones who had swooped me and caused Lanir to laugh when I screamed. He waited until they were closer, grabbed my face, and pointed to their beaks, too small to swallow even a finger.

A herd of the little goat animals moved about in the distance, and I pointed to them, but Lanir shook his head, indicating the trees.

Oh, so maybe we were going to get something other than meat today. Nice.

Enthusiastically, I nodded, and this time, instead of stumbling over the rocks before they flattened out, I grabbed Lanir's arm. He looked startled at the contact, but when I didn't release him, he started walking, relaxing into my touch as we moved. At the base of the mountain, instead of heading toward the field, we made our way toward the wooded area. The soil changed from rocky and mossy to almost sand-like, and before I stepped onto it, Lanir grabbed my arm and halted me.

He said something in his language, and I stared blankly at him. "Um, was that a warning of some sort?"

How was I supposed to know what he was saying?

Before Lanir stepped onto the sandy soil, he poked his spear against it, shuffling it around, then took a step. He then pointed to where he had stepped and then at me.

Understanding, I nodded and made sure I stepped exactly where he had.

So, there were monsters under the soil. *Great.* Part of me was curious about what other creatures this planet held, but maybe I didn't want to know. We made it only a few steps before reaching the first tree, and Lanir handed me his spear before he reached up, grabbed a strip of the bark, and pulled. The muscles in his arms rippled with the effort, and I raised my eyebrows. This wasn't something I would be able to do without his help.

"Isn't that the plant we start fires with?" The word *fire* triggered some understanding in him, and he made a twisting motion with his hands. "Oh, brilliant, so what do w… *ew!*" Lanir took a bite of the bark and chewed vigorously before offering it to me. "Uh…" I took the piece he offered and tried to bite into it as he had, but it was like biting into a strip of rubber. Instead, I nibbled at it with my front teeth. "Hmm…" I mumbled. "Not bad, almost nutty." Lanir seemed pleased with my assessment. "Shall I get the next one?" I offered, stepping to the side.

With a roar, Lanir shouldered me, sending me flying against the nearest tree. I clutched my head and groaned, fear spiking inside my chest. Lanir had never hurt me before. Did I do something to upset him? Blinking rapidly, I looked up. Lanir lifted his foot from the sand, and I caught a glimpse of a barb retreating before it disappeared.

"Oh my God, Lanir, I'm so sorry." I'd forgotten about whatever it was under the soil he had warned me about, and in his desperation to protect me, he'd been stabbed by something.

Maybe even poisoned.

And it was my fault.

I rushed to his side. *Was he going to die now?* I'd be alone on an alien planet and the death of an innocent being on my mind. "Lanir!" I cried out when he swayed dangerously and gripped a tree. He lifted his head, his eyes glazed, and snarled at me, reaching out and shoving me again.

Even poisoned, he was still trying to get me out of danger.

There was a sound that made my skin crawl, like a hundred rattlesnakes moving all at once. The soil started to shake, and slowly, creatures emerged, about the size of a football and a dark reddish brown, almost like giant crickets but with no wings and giant pincers. I screamed, and Lanir stumbled forward, again shoving me back. Taking the hint, I turned and ran back toward the foot of the mountains.

Turning, Lanir was a few steps behind me, his movements sluggish and staggered, and with another snarl, he collapsed against the rocks.

CHAPTER 10

SAMARA

"Lanir!" I cried out.

But his unconsciousness was only part of my problem—the evil creatures from the sand were approaching, and I looked around wildly for something to use as a weapon. I snatched the knife from Lanir's belt, holding onto hope as I heard him groan when I did so, and lunged toward where the creatures approached in a wave. Screaming with tears streaming down my face, I stabbed one of them and shrieked louder when a blast of greenish-gray blood and innards spurted out of it. When it died, it made a horrible gurgling and squealing sound, and the other creatures halted.

"*Back.* Get back!" I swung the knife at them, and they watched me wearily with their four beady black eyes.

They retreated, and I didn't relax until they had disappeared back under the sand. Apparently, they wanted easy prey, an unconscious meal to devour, and wouldn't fight for it.

Dropping to my knees, I ran my hand over Lanir's exposed cheek, his face pressed into the warmth of the rock. "Lanir, Lanir? Can you hear me?"

He groaned, and my breath hitched.

He was alive.

The horrible little creatures didn't come back, but who knew what other things this planet was hiding? I hadn't seen anything that seemed too dangerous, but what if that was because Lanir was always around? With him practically unconscious, they might all come out to attack him and eat me.

I shuddered. I needed to get Lanir to the cave.

With a herculean effort, I ducked down and lifted one of his arms over my shoulders. His arm felt like it weighed a ton, and I almost burst into tears from the effort. Was he *made* of stone as well as looking like it?

"*Lanir!*" I cried out, dropping his arm and shaking his shoulder. "I can't do this without you.

You have to help me." I couldn't leave him to die and flee myself. He'd taken me in and looked after me, and now I needed to look after him.

If I could only get him back to the cave.

Lanir groaned again and shifted, pushing himself up onto his knuckles and knees. He grumbled something, a stream of beautiful syllables that meant nothing to me, but I simply prayed they meant *I'm okay, I'll be okay.* He managed to stand but swayed dangerously, and I moved to his side, wanting to help. Lanir looked toward me, but his eyes were unfocused. He tried to lift his arm from my shoulders and muttered something else, but I held onto his wrist. "Let me help," I said, still struggling to hold back tears.

His first step was shaky, and his weight fell on my shoulder. I cried out, biting my lip too late to hold back the cry of pain. He was so heavy, and my knees buckled, twisting my ankle awkwardly on the rocks. Lanir looked at me again, snarling, and once again tried to lift his arm off my shoulders. Insistently, I grabbed his wrist again. He finally decided to stop arguing, and with lopsided and stumbling steps, we made our way slowly back to the cave. It took much longer than usual, even considering Lanir had earlier walked slower so I could keep up.

I'd witnessed how fast he could move if he wanted to.

It felt like hours. My mouth was dry, and I was desperate for a drink, but I almost cried with relief when I saw the cave's opening in the distance.

We were so close.

The moment we crossed the threshold into the cave, Lanir collapsed, pulling me down with him. I unhooked his arm from me and rolled out from underneath him, panting. Crawling to the water bag, I took a grateful few mouthfuls and gasped loudly. There was a thump behind me as Lanir dragged himself toward the pile of furs in the corner and collapsed onto his back in a partially seated position. He indicated his mouth and murmured something. Taking the hint, I moved to his side and held the water bag by his lips, squeezed it slowly and helped him to take some sips. Lanir muttered something else, the grumble of his words rumbling through his chest. I sat beside him, stroking his hand as his gaze slid to mine, and he watched me.

"You're going to be okay, right?" My lip trembled, and I shifted my gaze from his face to watch my fingers trace circles on the back of his large hand. "You saved me, and now you're hurt because of me. If you die because of me... I..." I pressed my fingers to my lips, failing to stop them trembling. "Just be okay, all right?"

His throat worked like he was trying to talk, but I shushed him gently, swiping away the tears on my cheeks. "Rest now. I'll take care of you."

He almost smiled, although it could have been a snarl, and his eyelids drooped before he fell asleep.

Lanir didn't wake, and after a couple of hours, I realized he might be hungry when he did.

Problem was, we had no food. We hadn't completed the hunt nor brought back any of that rubber bark. There was a bit in the cave, and now I had to decide whether to save it for eating or use it to start a fire.

My previous attempt to flee now seemed ridiculously foolish. I knew nothing of this place, and beyond that, I had no idea how to look after myself, let alone Lanir as well. But there was no point in me sitting here while he slept. I needed to do *something*.

Grabbing the water bags, I exited the cave and walked to the nearby creek to top them up. I took Lanir's spear with me, even though it was grossly oversized for me, but it felt wrong to leave without some sort of weapon. I filled the water bags and returned to the cave.

Now what?

I could try hunting. The idea made me cringe, but

I needed to act—anything to help. But the only other edible thing he'd shown me was the bark of those strange thin trees, and I wasn't going anywhere near that sandy soil again. I couldn't just grab some random plant and hope it was edible.

I felt useless.

Lanir was still sleeping, the rise and fall of his chest steady, which I hoped was a good thing. I checked his pulse, but there wasn't one on his neck. If I placed my ear to his chest, the steady drumming of his massive heart was clear. *Good*.

Exploring the cave, I found more of the rubber bark stuff, but not much. Despite my stomach growling in hunger, I decided not to eat any of it, saving a small amount to make a fire tonight and the rest for Lanir when he wakes up.

He'll need his strength back.

Too scared to go exploring by myself, I curled up next to Lanir and eventually fell into a troubled sleep.

My slumber was interrupted by howling winds, and I sat bolt upright. Lanir was somehow still sleeping or perhaps must still be unconscious. I couldn't imagine anyone sleeping through the ruckus that was created by the insane winds that now pummeled the cave. Everything was blowing around. The lighter things, like the fire kindling, were being swept across the ceiling and curved walls. I barely had time to duck as a bundle of twigs whooshed past my head before it collided with the cave wall, the neat bundle exploding open. The furs Lanir laid on flapped around, slapping his arms and legs and being noisier than I would have thought possible for animal hides. The only reason they weren't part of the whirlwind in the cave was his weight on them, but everything else, his neatly placed and cared-for items, were in disarray.

I ran my fingers through my hair, gripping briefly while I tried to think straight. This was my fault for not putting the animal skin in front of the door. But how was I supposed to know there'd be a mini tornado tonight? Or does this happen every night? Desperate but also cautious that he needed rest, I half-heartedly shook Lanir, torn between leaving him to recover and needing his help. He didn't wake anyway, and I hated the whimper that escaped my lips.

He'd protected me, and now I needed to protect him. I hadn't been able to hunt or gather food, so the very least I could do was fix this mess. This only reminded me I wasn't a strong person, and I wasn't a protector or carer. I wasn't the one who took charge and made things happen. I was a follower, a helper, who stood quietly in the corner and watched the world go by, completely content and happy in my own world.

But there was no help now. There was no one I could call and ask, no waiting for someone else to take the reins.

There was only Lanir, who had fallen ill because he tried to protect me.

Sniffing, I wiped my face, unaware when I had started crying. I hadn't realized how much I relied on someone else taking charge until I was truly alone.

I stood, flexing my hands and trying to urge myself to act before I shielded my eyes with my arm from the dust and debris and made my way to the cave's entrance. The cave was well-lit, and glancing outside, I gasped at the size of the moon, taking up a good chunk of the night sky in its bright glory, a calm feature when the world below it was in chaos. In the distance, the sea churned, the waves crashing over each other. I could almost hear it in my mind and shuddered to think what it would be like to be in those waters. The trees below the mountain were thrashing about wildly, and a howling was coming from the mountain itself, the winds working their way through the cave's system.

Wrapping my arms around my chest, I stepped back inside.

The covering Lanir had previously used to block

the opening was wedged between some rocks against the wall and moved out of the way, almost like a sliding door. Steeling myself, I pushed *hard* against the nearest rock and was rewarded with the scrape of it against the ground. But it only moved a matter of inches, and I wanted to cry out in frustration. I had no chance of moving the larger rocks, but if I could at least secure the screen with the smaller ones, then hopefully, we could safely make it through the night, and I could clean up before Lanir woke.

Achingly slow, I managed to move the rocks to either side of the entrance, creating a space to trap the canvas between them. My arms felt like jelly, and my feet were rubbed raw from constantly slipping on the rocky cave floor. I was sobbing by the time I was ready to move the animal skin into place, dust in my eyes and my hair a knotted mess, more than it already was. I wanted to go to Lanir again, shake him harder until he woke, beg him to help me, and tell him I couldn't do this without him.

But he wouldn't understand me anyway, and if he weren't already angry at getting poisoned because of me, he surely would be at the state his home was in now.

I'd let him down.

The realization I'd relied so heavily on Lanir until this point hit me like a ton of bricks, and my knees almost buckled under the sense of hopelessness as it threatened to overtake me. But there wasn't time for that. I had to be stronger. Gritting my teeth, I tugged the stiff covering from its storage space and wedged it between the rocks, finally sighing loudly when it was done as I choked back another sob. Lanir had built some sort of frame and stretched the animal skin around it, so it was like moving a giant painting. Stable, at least, but not easy to maneuver. The wind was slowly cut off, and I clambered over the rocks after securing a top corner in the cracks. It wasn't how he did it, but it would have to do. Yelping as I cut my foot, I stumbled the last few steps back to the cave floor, lifting my foot so I could see the damage. It didn't look too bad, and tentatively, I put some weight on it.

Once the barrier was in place, although I could still hear the howling of the wind around the exposed edges, at least it was better. Was it like this every night? Was the screen not so much to keep me from escaping but to keep me safe?

I glanced over at Lanir, and a wave of affection crashed over me. What was I to him? Why was he protecting me like this to the point he had sacrificed his safety to stop me from getting hurt?

With another sob, I moved over to where Lanir lay and bent, brushing my fingers along his cheek gently. He grumbled in his sleep, and I withdrew my hand, not wanting to disturb him. He wasn't so bad, and I hated that my doubt and self-preservation had made me question his intentions. Wasn't I better than this? Always seeing the best in others? He could've killed me, used me for food like the little fluffy goat creatures. But instead, he protected me, and I hated that I couldn't ask him why.

Or say thank you.

Straightening, I reorganized Lanir's belongings the best I could with the diminished light and returned everything to their rightful places before curling up next to him again. My chest to Lanir's side, I tucked myself against his large form and watched him sleep for a while. His strange dark gray and reddish skin seemed less alarming to me now, and I found myself longing for him to make that frustrated huff he does when I didn't understand something.

I almost smiled at the thought and touched his cheek again.

"Thank you," I whispered. I knew he couldn't hear me, and even if he could, he wouldn't understand, but I needed him to know I understood he had saved me and I appreciated him.

I just hoped he would wake and be okay, and if I couldn't tell him how I felt, maybe I could show him. Tracing my thumb along his bottom lip, his heavy brow drew into a frown, and I smiled. Leaning forward, I planted a soft kiss against his lips before curling up and going to sleep.

I would *show* him thank you in the morning.

CHAPTER II

LANIR

My body ached and felt as though it was heavier than I was used to. I shifted a shoulder, wanting to lift my arm. The weight of my healing body slowed me, and I snarled. I felt weakened, and I hated it. My tongue was thick in my mouth.

I was thirsty and hungry and *weak*.

I gave an experimental curl of my fingers.

And felt soft skin.

Startling, I glanced down, groaning as my head throbbed behind my eyes at the sudden movement. S'mara was curled up next to me, tucked into a small ball. Her skin and thin clothes were caked in dirt, and her hair was a knotted bundle at the base of her neck. Taking a visual sweep of the cave, it was covered in dust, and while my supplies were stacked neatly against the opposite wall, I immediately realized what had happened. The winds are savage at night, every night, and if I were unconscious, I wouldn't have been able to put the cover over the cave's entrance.

I'd failed S'mara. I hadn't looked after her properly nor protected her sufficiently. She'd suffered through the night without food, water, or shelter.

Rolling my head to the side, I noticed the screen was up. S'mara must've managed to move it, but only barely. It had shifted throughout the night and was at an odd angle. I was quietly impressed tiny S'mara had managed to get it set up at all. My chest swelled at the idea she had tried to protect me. I didn't remember lying down on the furs and animal skins, yet somehow, I was here. Had she dragged me?

When I tried to sit up, S'mara mumbled in her sleep and reached out, grabbing my upper arm and curling her arms around it.

So small, so fragile. She needed protecting.

I had to be able to talk to her.

Slowly, so as not to wake her, I rolled over so she was curled against me. A growl rumbled through my chest, and she moaned in her sleep again, causing me to still. The feel of her small body curled against me surged the possessiveness in me again. Her scent was too much. Beyond the dirt and sweat, she was… S'mara.

And I needed more.

Snarling again, I hated that I couldn't control my instincts better. I loathed them. The instinct to mate was a part of me the Ghaal designed when they wanted to use us, and I didn't want them to be such a strong force in who I was. But simply having S'mara near was enough to have my cock throbbing with need, even though my body still ached from the venom. The thought of claiming her took over everything else, and the need to mate was as strong as my need to survive.

But while I hated the instincts, I almost groaned at the feel of S'mara as she shuffled next to me in her sleep, rubbing against my cock through my loincloth. I imagined her small hand curling around my cock and gritted my teeth.

No. *Focus.*

Shoving down the feeling, I placed my fingers gently on her head and forged a connection.

S'mara's eyes shot open, and she cried out, "Lanir!" Her arms flew up and slapped against my chest, trying to grip and hold on to me or push me away, I wasn't sure.

I used my other arm to pull her against me,

holding her still as I connected my mind to hers, learning her language. Her eyes closed, and her pupils shifted wildly back and forth as she moaned again. How much could she take? Enough time and I could learn everything about her and her world, but I only needed enough to be able to speak to her.

I stopped, breaking the connection, and S'mara slumped in my arms, her breathing shallow. There was no pain. I wouldn't have done it if it caused her any pain, but it was an intense experience and drained her energy quickly. Snarling again, I felt selfish. She would be hungry and thirsty, and in my failure to provide, she went to bed without food. This was an ill-opportune time to learn her language, but she was so close, and she had almost been killed. I couldn't risk it. We needed to talk.

S'mara lifted a hand to her head, rubbing her forehead and frowning. "What was that? What did you do to me?" I didn't let her go as she blinked through her confusion. I didn't want to let her go ever—her body felt perfect curled up against mine, and I wanted *more.* It was the wrong time, but I couldn't help giving myself a moment to enjoy the heat of her against me, her small breasts pressed against my chest, the curve of her spine under my hand, and my fingers splayed on her back.

"What did you do to me, Lanir?" she whispered again, and I pulled her against me tighter.

"I'm sorry," I finally grumbled out the words,

rolling the unfamiliar and disjointed syllables around my tongue, my body automatically responding and adjusting to the new language. "I needed to be able to talk to you."

There was a moment of silence and then a gasp as S'mara slapped her palms against my chest and pushed. Reluctantly, I let her shift away slightly so she could look at my face. I couldn't help the growl that escaped me at the loss of contact.

"You speak my language," she cried out, her expression somewhere between disbelief and elation.

"I do now. I learned." I reached up and brushed my fingers against her temple, pleased when she didn't flinch or stop me from touching her. "I'm sorry. I wanted your permission before I made the connection, but we needed to be able to communicate."

"Yeah, no, yeah, of course." Her words were a jumble. She exhaled loudly and brushed her fingers against my hand, where I still touched her. "But why didn't you do it sooner?" I frowned, and she met my eyes. "Why didn't you just... like grab me and do it the moment I got here?"

I snorted, my eyes flashing dangerously. "I didn't have your permission. It'd be wrong."

"Aw," she whispered, tilting her head into my hand and giving me a small smile. Another growl rumbled through me, and her gaze was drawn to my chest at the sound before she looked back at my face. "That's sweet."

I didn't know what to say, so I said nothing. There was so much I needed to tell her about the dangers of this place and why she was here. About who and what I was and how it would be better if we moved from this cave. I wanted to apologize for failing her and letting her go hungry.

And to tell her about how my body and mind responded to her, how much I needed her, how she consumed my thoughts more and more with every day that passed, and that I knew it was wrong, but I couldn't help it. Maybe if she understood about me and knew I cared, she would look beyond my appearance, different from hers, and welcome me into her sweet cunt.

But any words right now would break the trance, and S'mara was still leaning into my touch. With a gentle stroke, I moved my thumb across her cheek. Her skin was so soft—I'd never felt anything like it before. The Ghaal's and my skin was rough and textured as was most of the animals here too. But S'mara was gentle, perfect, and needed my protection as much as I desired to protect her. Hesitantly, I touched her bottom lip, not wanting to push her but desperate to keep touching her.

Her lips trembled, her gaze never leaving mine, and S'mara placed her palms on my chest again, her lips curving into a shy smile when the contented growl started again.

"Thank you," she whispered, and I frowned.

"Why are you thanking me?"

She almost smiled again. "For saving me, keeping me safe, and feeding me." She broke eye contact only long enough to glance around the cave. "I'm sorry your cave is a mess. The winds were crazy. I tried to fix it." When she looked back at me, her eyes shined with unshed tears. "I also wanted to hunt. I didn't want you to wake with no food, but I was scared. I'm sorry. After those things in the ground, I didn't know what else was out there. I wanted to be here to make sure you were okay, and I was torn and didn't know what to do, so in the end, I did nothing. And I'm *so* sorry you got hurt trying to protect me. I'd never have forgiven myself if you'd been killed—"

"S'mara," I grumbled her name out, effectively cutting off her monologue. She looked at me with wide eyes, and I didn't know what she was waiting for me to say, if anything. But we held each other's eye contact for a moment, which seemed to be enough for now. There were so many words I wanted to say I didn't know where to start. So, I simply touched her more. I wanted to pull the rags off her body and drive my cock into her waiting cunt. Once again, the mental image of her under me distracted me, and S'mara gasped when I pressed my thumb against her lip and dipped my thumb slightly into her mouth, warm and wet and waiting. My other hand drew her closer to me. Her scent changed, and I growled again.

She was *aroused,* and I wanted more.

With a snarl, I shifted forward, pushing my face into the crook of her shoulder and neck, and I inhaled deeply. S'mara shuddered, and I still needed more.

More.

I traced my fingers down her neck, and she whimpered as I cupped my palm over her breast.

"S'mara," I grumbled her name, marveling at how small she felt under my hands.

More.

Her scent called to me, her arousal increasing, and I wanted to taste her.

I moved my hand farther down and slipped it under her clothes, intrigued when I found a small patch of hair between her legs. She gasped my name, and her fingers curled against my chest, her breathing rapid. She didn't ask me to stop, but we hadn't spoken much yet, and I should ask for her permission.

I should stop and communicate with her, tell her everything she needed to know.

But I didn't want to stop.

Dipping a finger between the lips of her cunt, I growled when I found she was already wet for me. The scent of her cunt increased, and I snarled again, dragging my tongue up her neck and under her chin. I wanted to bite, but she was so delicate, so I settled for licking again, wanting to taste her skin under the layer of dirt, and when I did, I groaned, my cock straining against my loincloth.

"Lanir," S'mara gasped when I moved my hand lower, desperate to touch her more. The pad of my finger was at the entrance to her cunt, and she trembled in my arms. When I pushed ever so gently, wanting to feel the slick heat of her squeeze around my finger, she breathed out, "*Wait.*"

I stopped, my arm shaking with the effort of remaining still. "S'mara?" I growled out.

"I, uh…" She buried her face against my chest and mumbled something.

"I didn't hear you," I said, unable to stop swirling my finger lightly around her entrance, soaking my finger with her body's juices.

"I've never done this before." She swallowed, looking up but not meeting my eye. "I'm a virgin."

It took a moment for her words to register, and as I withdrew my hand from between her legs, I couldn't help but drag my finger up her cunt, relishing in the squeak she released as my finger passed over the small bump near the top of her cunt. I was battling against my instinct that was raging harder and stronger ever since I had seen S'mara.

But knowing she was untouched, that no other

male had been between her soft thighs...

... I liked that, and the growl rumbled harder in my chest.

She was trembling, her face still pressed against my chest, and my brow furrowed. "Are you okay?"

"I'm embarrassed."

"Why? You've been waiting for me."

She peeled herself back and looked into my eyes. "What do you mean?"

"You've been saving your cunt for only my cock to give you pleasure."

"*Oh my God,*" she muttered, a pink flush creeping over her cheeks. She cleared her throat, patting me gently on my chest. "We... uh, have a lot to talk about."

"Can it wait until after I fuck you?" The boldness of my words surprised even me, and S'mara's cheeks flushed brighter.

"I think we should talk first." My initial reaction was frustration at her words, but I pushed that to the side and leaned back so I could study S'mara's face. She'd allowed me to touch her, had responded to my touch, and I wanted more. She did too. I needed to be patient and held back a snarl. Patience was not something I was good at, but for her, I would try harder.

S'mara stayed curled in my arms, her hands on my chest and fingers tracing patterns against my skin. "How can you now speak to me?" Her expression showed only interest, not fear, and for this, I was thankful. Tentatively, I reached out and brushed my fingers along her hip. S'mara said nothing, but her cheeks flushed pink again. She didn't stop me, so I let my hand rest there while I answered her.

"I'm an adaptive species… a Synth, and can learn languages through connecting my mind to others." I waved a hand carelessly over my body. "I look the way I do because I adapt to my environment. The mountains, the lava holes, the ash… this is why I am the way I am."

"Are you alone here?"

"I have you," I grumbled, squeezing her hip again and pulling her toward me, pressing my hard cock against her stomach. The knowledge that no male had touched her before only surged me forward more. S'mara was mine to claim, to bring pleasure, to make my own. I will make her come so she's wet, and her cunt is begging to be filled by me.

She giggled. "Okay, Mr. Flirt, I'm going to need you to tone it down until I've learned what I need to know. We can't all learn just by touching heads, you know?" She brushed playfully at my hand on her hip, but instead of pushing it away, she rested her hand on top of mine. She seemed more comfortable around me than she had since she arrived. Was this purely because we could speak now? I'd displayed weakness by being taken down by the eylak venom, and yet she was closer to me now, physically and otherwise, than she had been.

It almost seemed she cared for my well-being. But surely that's only because she needed me to survive so I could take care of her? I was alien to her, probably a monster. Physically larger with tougher skin, she had more fingers than me, and they were slender and delicate like the rest of her. Fingers topped with tiny nails that couldn't even be called claws. But she had wide child-bearing hips, and I liked that. I must look like a monster to her. Yet she let me touch her the way she did. I didn't know what to think. The reawakening of my mating instincts was muddling my thoughts, and touching her was distracting, but I couldn't stop.

But S'mara wanted answers and information, and I owed them to her. I needed to concentrate.

"I meant..." she continued, holding my eye contact, "... do you have any family? Are there any others like you?"

"I have five brothers. But we are adaptive and live apart. They would no longer look like me."

"Why don't you live together?"

I hesitated. There wasn't really any line of questioning that *wouldn't* lead down the path requiring me to tell S'mara about the Ghaal. I hated the idea of sullying her mind with such a horrible reality, but she deserved to know.

"S'mara..." I mumbled, squeezing her hip again,

"… there is so much to tell you."

"So, tell me," she whispered.

She made it sound so simple, and I guessed it was. I didn't want to tell her, not yet or ever, if I could avoid it. I only wanted to take her away and keep her safe, but that was my instinct talking, not my mind, and she deserved to know.

"There's another species here, the Ghaal, and they seek to harm you."

"Me? What did I do?"

I shook my head. "You did nothing wrong. But you are physically compatible with the Ghaal. They are a dying species, and in their desperation to rekindle their population, they have searched other planets for species they can use for breeding."

The color drained from S'mara's face. "You mean, they intend to use me… to use *us*…" She didn't need to say it, and I didn't need to explain further, so I simply nodded. S'mara shuddered and shuffled forward, bringing her closer and pressing her body against mine. "You saved me from them, right? You're keeping me safe?"

A growl rumbled through my chest, and S'mara jumped slightly. "I'll protect you."

S'mara said nothing but pressed her forehead against my chest. I could feel the muscles of her face moving against my skin as she worked her way through this information. She'd been taken from her home, like many others before her, to be used as nothing more than a science experiment, a being with no rights and only a useable womb.

The growl in my chest increased with my rage, and startled S'mara looked up.

"I'm sorry," I muttered, holding her still in case she tried to move from me. "The idea of the Ghaal trying to… of what they've done before…" I couldn't get the words out or even consider what would happen if they got their hands on her. The image of the female's body Ilk and I had found and what the Ghaal did to her filled my mind again.

It never really left.

But S'mara was mine.

Mine.

I couldn't protect the human females who came before her, the ones the Ghaal captured that had proven to them humans were a compatible species.

The females they tore apart to make sure they had it right…

I couldn't save them. But S'mara, I would save her.

"What about the others?" she whispered.

"Others?"

"The other girls who were dropped here with me. Erica, Misha, Tori? Have you seen them? Are they safe? Or have the Ghaal got…" She choked back the emotion, and I pulled her against me.

"My brothers would be protecting them."

Even as I said it, I hoped it wasn't a lie.

CHAPTER 12

SAMARA

It was strange talking to Lanir as though we hadn't spent the last few days fumbling around each other, trying to communicate. All this time, all he needed was a minute or two to touch my head, and he could've learned my language. But he didn't want to touch me without permission. The thought swelled my heart with gratitude and sympathy. It must have been so frustrating for Lanir to know that we *could* talk to each other, but being unable to communicate the process to me because humans didn't have anything similar.

The magnitude of his patience and kindness hit me harder. All the things he had done and the frustration of trying to cross language and species barriers when, all along, the solution was *right there.* It turns out I was right to trust him. Of course, I had doubts and fears and even toyed with plans of escape, but I needed to remember who *I* was. I was someone who trusted their gut, and who, admittedly, while I could be naïve, generally got a good read on people after having learned a few hard lessons. Lanir was protecting me all along. He had more than enough opportunities to hurt me but didn't.

And beyond that, he was waiting for my *consent* to touch me to learn my language. How could I not feel even safer knowing that? But the past didn't matter now—we were communicating.

And he kept *touching me.*

Once the barrier of him being unsure if he could touch me or not was broken, he couldn't *stop* touching me. I mean, he stopped if I told him to when I confessed I was a virgin, and it felt wonderful to feel safe and in control like that. But now he was almost always touching me in some way—a hand on my shoulder or lower back, a brush of the arm, and when he was feeling daring, he'd brush his thumb across my lower lip, his eyes darkening in a dangerous way that sent a wave of warmth between my thighs.

Lanir literally looked like a demon, minus the horns and tail. He was everything I was raised to fear, and yet whenever I looked at him, and he looked at me like I was the most delicious thing he'd ever seen, my only reaction was arousal.

It was distracting, but I didn't want him to stop.

Only yesterday, I thought I'd lost him, that he was going to die in his sleep because he had tried to save me. At first, I thought it was simply fear of being alone on an alien planet that drove my compassion. But seeing Lanir lying there unconscious, I realized it was something more. I *cared* about him, and apparently, he did me too.

As if Lanir shoving me out of the way and taking some alien poison in the foot wasn't proof enough he cared.

He said there was another alien race here, wanting to find me and the other girls to use as some sort of breeding machines, and Lanir was protecting me. I shuddered and pressed myself against him again as we sat by the fire, cooking the meat Lanir had hunted. We'd filled the water bags, and after a drink, I was feeling better, but the smell of cooking meat had my mouth watering.

Lanir poked the meat on the hot rocks with a stick, and after a moment of hesitation, he wrapped an arm around my body and pulled me next to him. Perhaps it was wrong of me to press against him like this, but I needed comfort, and Lanir was the most comforting being I'd ever been around. He made me feel safe in an unknown world.

I had so many more questions, but right now, I simply needed to be held. We talked just enough to realize we were both hungry and thirsty, and I'd fussed over him and wanted to make sure his head didn't hurt after he'd clutched it when he sat up. Lanir also said he'd make me some new clothes, and while I was excited about getting out of these and bathing, the idea of being naked around Lanir filled me with conflicting emotions I couldn't even begin to unpack right now.

Lanir handed me some cooked meat, and his deep voice rumbled through me as he asked, "Do you have any other questions?"

"So, so many," I admitted, crushing myself against him further, if it was at all possible, pressed as I was against his side. "But right now, I just want to sit, cuddle, and eat if that's okay."

Lanir grunted in what I hoped meant it was okay and kept his arm around me as we ate.

His touching me earlier had turned me on more than I thought it would. After we'd eaten, I wanted to close my eyes and fall asleep in his arms and hope I felt better and my mind was clearer when I woke.

But I wasn't tired.

Instead, I wanted to explore the body of the being next to me. We were alone, and what did I have to lose? There was a lot more I needed Lanir to tell me, but in this moment, I only wanted to run my fingers over his chest.

So, I did. Reaching over and turning him to me, I then climbed onto his lap.

The deep growling started again in Lanir's chest. It was strange. It seemed he did it when he was both angry and happy—sometimes a growl and sometimes closer to a heavy purr. His skin was strange too, feeling like it was always covered in a fine sheen of dust but hard as stone. A dark, ashy gray coupled with the red splashes certainly made the idea of him being a demon hard to shake, but his green eyes broke the trance, and his face, despite the size difference, looked almost human.

I kept exploring his chest and arms with my fingers, and Lanir didn't move, allowing me to touch him. I moved up to feel his cheek gently before moving to his lips as I had the night before.

Lanir's lips were firm, but not hard like the ridges of his chest or nose. His tongue was a deep gray like the rest of him, and when he darted it out and licked his lips, I found myself wanting to caress it. I still wanted to thank him for saving me and sticking by me even when I tried to escape or made life difficult for him. There weren't enough words, and I hoped I wouldn't offend him by asking.

"Can I kiss you?" This wasn't like me—I never instigated. But being near Lanir and knowing anything could happen at any time, and I'd already almost lost him once, made me bolder than ever before. I felt safer in the arms of this alien than I had any other time. The danger to me was greater on this planet than on Earth, but I knew Lanir would protect me.

Lanir frowned. "I know the word because of your language, but I've never done it."

"Never? You don't have kissing here?" It was so strange to think I might be more experienced than someone in something sexual.

Lanir pressed his lips together. "The Ghaal have hard lips and do not kiss."

"But, you're not a Ghaal?" I questioned, and Lanir shook his head, watching my lips.

"I am adaptive—"

"You adapt to your environment, I remember. But why would that change your face? Did you used to have hard lips?"

"The Ghaal didn't want us to be too similar to them, since they saw themselves as superior. We were useful to them to breed and nothing more."

"Hmm," I hummed out, brushing past his lips again. "I guess we have that in common." When I licked my upper lip before running my teeth along the bottom one, Lanir groaned. "So, would you mind if I kissed you?"

"You can do anything to me."

I chuckled, touching his nose. "Ah-ah, we know consent is important." Lanir frowned, then his lips curved into almost a smile when he realized I was teasing him. His smile faded when I moved closer, his hands gripping my hips harder. "Just follow my lead."

It felt incredible to be taking charge, to have this hulking great alien under me, ready to learn how to kiss. I was filled with a sense of power even though he dwarfed me, and I smiled before closing my eyes, opening them just to make sure Lanir had his closed too.

When I pressed my lips to his, he growled again.

He stayed still, the growl rumbling through his chest, his lips and mouth unmoving under my ministrations. I tried to coax him into moving by running my tongue along his lips, and when he didn't, I pulled away. His eyes were lit with intensity, and his fingers gripped me as if he were afraid I was going to leave entirely.

"Did I do something wrong?"

I chuckled. It was such an innocent question, and to be coming from a demon-looking alien made it even more obscure. My laughter made him quirk a brow, not understanding the joke. "No," I said, soothing him, running a hand down his hard chest. "Nothing wrong. Just move your lips against mine, and when you're comfortable, open your mouth." He tilted his head slightly to the side, and I almost grinned at the innocence of the gesture. "Then I can massage my tongue against yours."

This ushered another groan from him, but dutifully, he closed his eyes and leaned forward slightly. Cupping his cheek in my hand, I closed the gap and again pressed my lips to his. This time, when I ran my tongue over his lips, he opened his mouth, inviting me in. His tongue was harder than I was expecting, almost like it had an exoskeleton of its own. But because it was Lanir, and he was the one I wanted to kiss, I kept going, massaging his tongue gently with mine.

The rumble in his chest increased, and he grabbed the back of my head, tilting my face to give him better access to my mouth as he took control of the kiss. My eyes flew open for a moment before fluttering closed in ecstasy as he kissed me. Adaptive didn't cover it. He learned quickly. Lanir drove his tongue into my mouth, exploring mine and thrusting in slightly. I moaned into his mouth, and his grip on my already knotted hair increased.

I pulled back, gasping for air, and looked at Lanir, heavy-lidded. "Wow, you *are* a fast learner."

"I understand the appeal," Lanir rumbled out, still gazing at me with lust. "It's like how I would tongue-fuck your cunt."

"Oh my God..." I whispered, my mouth suddenly dry.

He tilted his head again but said nothing more and simply let a menacing grin spread across his

face like he wanted to eat me alive.
    In a way, I guess he did.

CHAPTER 13

LANIR

S'mara and I spent the remainder of the day stocking up the cave with food and water and rewrapping the kindling bundles that had been damaged when the cave wasn't protected from the night winds. It was nice doing the things I would do every day, but it was better with her. While I had my duty of protecting kidnapped species, I was merely existing between unit drops, not really living. Over time, I had lost who I was beyond the duty my brothers and I had sworn to. But having her with me, I was living again. I remember in the early days after we had escaped from the Ghaal, we'd play-fight and hunt together.

When we pretended we could live normal lives together.

Until we saw the units and knew everything had changed.

Sometimes, I wondered if we should have given in and let the Ghaal use us for breeding, then they would never have needed to search other planets for compatible species. But how could we give in knowing how violent they were and how they treated their females and each other? I couldn't— my conscience wouldn't allow it.

As much as my guilt plagued me, it was difficult to give in because if we hadn't followed the exact path we treaded, then I wouldn't have S'mara with me.

And I looked forward to the day when she felt comfortable enough to welcome me into her sweet, slick cunt. I'd be as gentle as I could, given how small and delicate she was. I'd make her come with my mouth before and make sure she was dripping with arousal to help take the girth of my cock.

I showed S'mara the gladvin roots—clear berry-like growths on the roots that gave a burst of sweetness when eaten, but the oils could also be used for cleaning. I'd promised to show S'mara where she could bathe and said I would make her some new clothes to replace the rags she currently wore. The list of things I needed to do for her was long, and I cursed myself inwardly, feeling like a failure. I had failed to look after her properly from the beginning. She should already have new clothes and a weapon and be clean with her hair braided. I didn't keep my braid, wanting no reminders of the Ghaal, but I remembered how to do them so her hair wouldn't get so knotty. She seemed pleased with this and smiled at me as we walked toward the warm springs, carrying a small handful of gladvin roots.

When we reached the springs, I led S'mara toward a large one that wouldn't be too deep for her. She stood on the edge, staring into the clear bubbling water, and bent a knee so she could dip her toes in. "It's warm," she said.

"Yes, the springs are kept warm by the lava."

"Right." She seemed unsettled, but after casting a nervous glance between the spring and me a few times, she decided to trust it and placed the roots on the ground. Standing, she faced me, her hands on the edges of the rags she wore, uncertain.

She was embarrassed. I realized too late, and the flush had already begun to creep up her cheeks.

"S'mara," I mumbled, shuffling my weight from foot to foot. "I apologize if you're embarrassed to be naked in front of me, but I'd rather not leave you alone. There are dangers out here, you understand?"

"Yes," she whispered, still fingering the edges of the thin material of her top. "I understand, but um… would you mind turning around until I'm in the water?"

I nodded, turned as she requested, and waited until I heard the water slosh against the sides of the spring and S'mara's hum of satisfaction. Turning back, her nudity was hidden from me by the edge of the spring and surrounding small rocks, and I sat on a nearby stone, pulling out the furs and skins I'd brought with me to begin sewing her new clothes. I got to work, glancing up intermittently to keep an eye on S'mara. Her head was tilted back, working the oils from the gladvin roots into her scalp and combing her fingers through her long hair, a look of pure bliss on her face.

Biting back a groan, I got back to work. I could see her neck and shoulders, and her skin glistened in the sunlight from the water and oils as she washed her hair. I wanted to help, to be the one to run my hands over her body, cupping her breasts and moving down to her ass. I'd easily be able to lift her and hold her against the edge of the spring and fuck her right there.

She looked up when I growled. "Lanir? Are you okay?"

"Yes." I pushed the word through gritted teeth, and when our eyes met, her cheeks flushed again. She knew. S'mara *knew* my attraction to her. Of course she did. I hadn't made a secret of it. But if I wanted her trust, I needed to keep myself under control.

It wasn't easy. My instincts had come to the surface now, and the scent of her skin, hair, and arousal wafted through the air between us. My body responded, desperate with a desire to claim her, to *mate*, to spill my seed inside her until she was round with my child.

I bit my tongue to cut off the groan that almost escaped and got back to work on S'mara's clothes, using hair from the flaxia and skin from an oarke to make her a slip. I wasn't as adept at sewing as some of my brothers, but I did the best I could, fashioning her a simple dress with a tie for her waist and some boots lined with fur to keep her feet safe. The ground was rough, and she was so soft. S'mara needed to be protected.

When her clothes were completed, I stood, the movement drawing S'mara's gaze to me.

"I'm almost done, I think," she said, tilting back and gliding through the water, her breasts peeking out the surface of the water, nipples hardening at the cool air. I tried not to look at the small pink nubs and managed to shift my gaze away moments before S'mara could become concerned at my attention.

She smiled at me. "I'll um... meet you back at the cave if you like?"

"No." The word came out harsher than I'd planned. S'mara shrank back, and her smile vanished. "I mean…" I tried to correct myself, twisting her new dress between my hands, "… I don't want to leave you alone."

Her expression softened. "I know, Lanir. But this isn't like the other day. The cave is just around the corner, and I need to dry myself. I'm… I'd just like a bit of privacy." When I continued to stare at her, she added, "Besides, if I'm going to learn to survive on this planet, I'm eventually going to need to be able to make the small journey from here to the cave, right?"

She was correct, and I scowled, unwilling to voice my confirmation. Striding to the spring, she recoiled slightly but didn't move away from the edge. I crouched at the side, dropped her new dress and shoes and a fur for her to dry herself beside the spring and snatched up her old clothes. Leaning forward, I ran my hand over her cheek.

"You will follow immediately, yes?"

"As soon as I'm dry and dressed, I'll be on my way. I promise."

With a snarl, I tilted her chin up to me. "Don't make me come looking for you."

Her lip quirked into almost a smile as if she would enjoy the game, and my cock stirred under my loincloth. I would leave, but I wouldn't go all the way back to my cave. I simply couldn't. I'd be right around the corner where she couldn't see me. I looked like my environment, and if I stayed still, I was almost invisible. I knew it was a betrayal of her trust, but S'mara obviously did *not* understand the dangers this place held. My gut twisted at the knowledge I would need to tell her we had to leave soon. In restocking the cave, I'd really been prepping for us to move on. It wasn't safe here.

S'mara would be safest if we kept moving.

After a short while, we would find Ilk and decide what to do.

Maybe he knew of her friends.

Nodding curtly, I stood and, against all my instincts, left S'mara alone.

True to her word, S'mara pulled herself from the spring and began to dry herself. She scrunched and twisted her long hair in her fingers until the water splashed onto the rocks. Her damp hair lay down her back, and I would braid it for her when we got back to the cave. It was a small thing, but I was already looking forward to the intimacy of the touch. Any excuse of contact with S'mara sent desire fueling through me.

The only thing keeping me back was repeating to

myself over and over—*soon.*

Soon, she would come to me.

I had to believe she would.

Otherwise, I feared my instincts would battle to overcome me. But I would die before I became as much of a danger to S'mara as the Ghaal were.

For now, I watched her body as she stood and stretched—the slight bulge of her rounded belly, the swell of her hips and thighs, and the delicious curve of her back. She was beautiful. Her eyes were large and innocent, and her hands and feet were small and delicate, as was the pinch of her waist.

Once dressed, S'mara turned and made her way toward me, so I ducked out of sight and clambered over and around the rock formations I knew so well so I'd make it back to the cave first, and she wouldn't know I'd been watching her at all.

CHAPTER 14

SAMARA

God, it felt so good to be clean.

My hair was still a bit knotty, but with the oils from the clear root berries—so large they took up almost my entire palm—I'd managed to work out most of the damage. Lanir said he'd braid my hair once I'd bathed, and I sighed. The idea of sitting there and letting his fingers work soothingly over my scalp sounded like heaven.

Halfway toward the first curve in the mountain, I stopped, swearing I'd heard footsteps.

Was Lanir still here, watching me? I wanted to be

angry at the thought, but the look on his face when I'd told him I wanted to walk alone was hard to get out of my head. He appeared absolutely devastated, but his jaw tensed as though he was fighting the urge to keep from arguing. It made total sense he would stay nearby to keep an eye on me—it was kind of sweet. But again, Lanir was trying to give me what I asked for, and I had to give him points for that.

Smiling, I called out, "Lanir? I know it's you. You can come out. I'm not mad."

I stood there grinning to myself for a moment like an idiot before a prickling at the back of my neck only served to increase my suspicion I was being watched. But not by Lanir. When he looked at me, I felt warm and safe, but even with the sun on my neck, a cold shiver worked its way up my spine. Already trembling, I turned around.

Strangers.

There were three of them, standing in a line, having come over the crest of the mountain. Their skin was gray, and they had lines of purple hair, so thick it was almost fur, trailing down the backs of their arms and neck to match their braids.

I managed to wrench my gaze away from their unsettling orange eyes and glanced at their mouths—their noses protruding and lips hard.

Ghaal.

"Lanir!" I shrieked, turned, and bolted toward

the cave.

The Ghaal came after me—their footsteps pounded against the mountainside and echoed in my ears. My mind screamed warnings at me that they were faster, stronger, and I was vulnerable. When I pushed myself harder and felt the brush of a hand at my shoulder, I prayed it was my imagination as they screeched something at me with their disjointed syllables, but I dared not turn around. I called out for Lanir again, wishing I hadn't sent him away. How stupid I was to assume I could look after myself for even a second on this strange planet when there were beings after me. I could only hope now my suspicions that Lanir hadn't truly left me alone were real.

Because if he had, I'm certain I was about to be taken.

I risked a glance back only to see one of the Ghaal raising a weapon of some kind. I screamed again, trying to move faster, but was hindered by the unfamiliar terrain and boots that weren't made for fleeing.

They don't want me dead.

They don't want me dead.

I told myself repeatedly, even as I heard the hum of their weapons warming up.

There was a small explosion, and I thought for a moment the sheer power of it had knocked me off my feet. But I couldn't move my legs, and looking down, something had clasped itself over the back of my thighs, almost like a giant mechanical crab. It was attached to a thin chain that straightened and became taut as the Ghaal stopped chasing me, instead using their trap to drag me back toward them. I cried out and attempted to grab every rock I passed but succeeded only in cutting up my hands as I was forced to let go each time, the mechanical crab locked hard onto my legs.

For a moment, I thought there was another explosion, the sound feeling like it rocked the ground.

It was a roar.

Lanir.

The Ghaal behind me shrieked and chattered amongst themselves as the chain pulling me moved faster before coming to an abrupt halt. The clasp around my legs was large, and although I tried tucking my legs under me to stand, I couldn't. I couldn't even bend my knees to crawl. Instead, I inched forward on my stomach, dragging myself with my fingers across the rocky outcrops. Heavy footsteps rang past me, and I caught a glimpse of deep gray and glowing red as Lanir went thundering toward the group of Ghaal.

Turning my head, I opened my mouth to scream as one of the Ghaal was practically on top of me. Over his shoulder, I could see Lanir. One Ghaal was on his back with his arm wrapped around Lanir's throat, and the other fiddled desperately with his weapon while Lanir struck out wildly in all directions. The one closest to me grabbed my hair and yanked my head back, and when I screamed and struggled, he shoved me. My forehead collided with the rocks, and my vision blurred as the ground splattered with blood.

Feeling woozy, I struck out blindly, whimpering and crying out for Lanir to help me.

Sickly hands clasped over my wrists as I continued to flail my arms about, refusing to make this easy for them. If they were going to take me, I was going down fighting. I would fight them every second of the way. I'd been compliant when I was abducted, but no more. The Ghaal who held me turned when a gut-churning cry was followed up with a crunching sound I feared I'd never get out of my head.

Lanir had broken the spine of a Ghaal over his knee.

The second one was backing up as Lanir approached him, having discarded the unresponsive weapon. Even from where I lay, I could see the rage in Lanir's eyes, the vivid green shining in the sunlight, and his knuckles cracking as he clenched and released his fists. The Ghaal said something to Lanir, holding up his hands in surrender, but there was no surrender. Lanir was too far gone past the point of reason, nothing more than an animal. He grabbed the Ghaal's shoulder, placed his other hand on the Ghaal's head, and with a twist and a lurch, broke his neck, the sound making me gag.

Before the Ghaal's body had even hit the ground, Lanir had turned toward the one who was still kneeling over me, who watched the slaughter with his orange eyes wide and fearful. He scrambled to his feet, dragging me with him, and wrapped his forearm around my neck as Lanir stalked toward us.

"Make him back off," the Ghaal hissed in my ear.

I froze, and Lanir's steps faltered. "I understood you."

"Make him back off," he repeated, his voice oddly scratchy like he was talking through an old record player.

"Lanir," I said as I held my hand in front of me. "Stop. Please."

Lanir halted with a scowl, blowing air through his nose as he huffed angrily. His gaze didn't move from the Ghaal behind my shoulder, his arms and shoulders tense. I wanted to run into his arms, ask him to hold me and tell me I was safe with him, and promise him I'd never do something so stupid again. I didn't belong alone on this planet, not while there were threats as big as an entire species after me to use me as a breeding machine. The thought made me shudder, and only then did Lanir's gaze shift to mine. A brief flash of concern passed across his eyes before the rage took over again.

"Release her," Lanir said, snarling, "Or I will tear you limb from limb."

"You come near me, and I'll break her neck like you did to Axka."

Lanir snarled. "You hurt her in any way, and you'll be *begging* for death by the time I'm done with you."

The Ghaal faltered for only a moment, and the realization hit me. He was *afraid* of Lanir. Not just for what he'd done today but genuine terror as though Lanir was a monster.

"You're afraid," I blurted out, trying to twist around to look at my attacker. "You're scared of him, aren't you?"

The Ghaal ignored me but stepped back, forcing my heels to drag on the rocks as I still couldn't bend my legs to step backward. Lanir sneered. "Yes, my mate, they are scared of me." His lip lifted further to reveal sharp teeth and black gums, his tongue darting out menacingly. "I am what they made me, after all."

The Ghaal almost tripped over. "You."

Lanir was stepping forward at the same rate the Ghaal was moving back, one step at a time, keeping the distance between us even, not allowing him to take me away.

I watched the exchange between them.

The Ghaal trembled with fear or rage or both, I couldn't tell. "You refused to do what you were designed for. Discipline was necessary."

"Your methods of *discipline* simply proved we were right in refusing to help you rebuild your vicious species!" Lanir roared so loud I flinched. "Let. Her. *Go.*"

"If I let her go now, more of us will come anyway. We know the humans are here, and we *will* get them." He hissed out something then in what I can only assume was his native language, and Lanir's eyes widened before he bared his teeth and growled.

Whatever he said was evidently the wrong thing.

Lanir launched forward, and the Ghaal snarled, shoving me toward Lanir. I reached out, losing my footing with my bound legs, and clutched clumsily onto Lanir's arm. In his rage, he released my hold on him, wrenching himself from my grip and grabbing my upper arm just enough to assist me to the ground.

When the Ghaal drew another weapon, fiddling with it again—*was all their technology this unreliable?*—Lanir released me, and I slipped, knocking my head against a rock as I fell.

Lying on the warm, ashy gray stone, breathing in the dust that smelled like smoke and earth, I watched as Lanir cornered the Ghaal, grabbed his arms, smashed his hand against the rocks, and forced him to release the useless weapon. The Ghaal hissed and spit words at Lanir, words I could barely hear or understand. His insults or pleads—whatever they were—turned to screams when Lanir grabbed his arms and yanked them in opposite directions, ripping them from the Ghaal's shoulder sockets and spraying the rocks and Lanir in murky gray blood.

My stomach churned at the violence of the sight in front of me.

As the Ghaal sank to his knees, Lanir placed a palm to his forehead, the image looking almost holy with the sun behind him, peeking over the rocks, as if Lanir was about to purge the demon from the being in front of him. But the moment was shattered as Lanir roared again and smashed the Ghaal's head against the rock behind him, completely pulverizing it, the headless body falling with an empty thunk onto the rocks.

I dry retched, and my head spun.

Lanir turned and ran toward me, his heavy footsteps the last thing I saw before I passed out.

CHAPTER 15

LANIR

The sun had set, and the moon was high in the sky before S'mara stirred. I'd hastily washed once I had her back in the safety of the cave and discarded the fur rags I'd used to hide the evidence of the Ghaal's gray blood that had coated my hands. I didn't want to frighten S'mara. When I'd turned after killing the final Ghaal, her eyes were on me and wide with fear before she'd lost consciousness.

The Ghaal had threatened her, telling me in detail of their plans to attempt to impregnate the human females *manually* before using technology.

Him telling me was nothing more than a power play, and he paid for his words with his life, though I had no doubt they would have followed through with the threat. There was no end to that scenario without death.

Either I'd kill any Ghaal who tried to take S'mara from me, or I'd die trying.

But they made us strong and agile, traits they wanted to pass on to their offspring. Their biggest mistake was giving my brothers and me minds of our own.

I felt no guilt for killing them, but I worried S'mara might be frightened of me again.

At least maybe now she wouldn't hate me when I told her we couldn't stay here.

The Ghaal knew the units had been dropped and roughly where. They'd been able to locate S'mara, so we needed to get moving, not staying in one place for more than a night or two. We'd move just long enough to throw them off her scent and trail. Their tracking equipment was old and breaking, much like everything else, and they had only their scout teams to find her.

Then we would find my brother, Ilk.

S'mara murmured under her breath, and I grabbed the water bag and sat next to her. With a damp rag, I wiped her forehead. I'd cleaned the dust from her arms, legs, and face once I got her back and cleaned the scratches on her hands and legs. None of them were deep, but a growl still rumbled through my throat at the thought of any injury she sustained because of them. The covering I'd put on the wound on her stomach had already fallen off, the wound now clean and covered with a fresh layer of skin.

The cut on her head was my fault. I let her go too abruptly in my haste to get to the Ghaal. She was my *mate*, although she wasn't ready to hear that yet. I was blinded by rage, by the all-consuming need to protect her that I hadn't accounted for how small and delicate she was when I let her arm go, higher off the ground than I'd anticipated. She hadn't been able to bend her legs and instead fell heavily.

The contraption on her legs had proven difficult to remove. But when my frustration took over, I managed to snap it at the hinge and free her. I tossed it into a lava pit on my way back here, S'mara curled up against my chest in my arms.

"S'mara," I murmured, offering her some water. I squeezed the bag gently, releasing a trickle of liquid onto her dry lips. Her small tongue darted out, and she hummed before opening her mouth. I pressed harder on the skin bag, and she drank a few mouthfuls before her eyes fluttered open.

"Lanir," she whispered, bringing me into focus.

When she said nothing further, my words caught in my chest. I was more than an alien to her—I was a monster. I'd kidnapped her, frightened her, and then showed her a violent side of me I never wanted to release again, especially not in front of a mate I never thought I'd have. It didn't matter she hadn't welcomed me between her legs yet. She was mine. I felt it.

Her brows furrowed together at my silence, and I reached out, cupping her cheek. She didn't flinch or pull away, and I almost cried with relief. "Do you hate me?" I asked.

Her eyes widened, and she tried to sit before clutching her head and allowing me to help her back down into the pile of furs. Keeping her eyes closed, she said, "Why would I hate you?"

"I killed those Ghaal."

When she opened her eyes, her gaze on me was intense. "You were saving me. *Again.*"

My brow drew down as I processed her words. S'mara didn't hate me and wasn't even mad at me. She knew I was only trying to protect her.

How could such a fragile and beautiful creature trust me?

"I can almost see you working through your thoughts." Her words broke me out of my trance, and when I looked at her, her lips were curved into a small smile. "You're not a monster, Lanir... not to me."

I didn't know what to say, so I simply grunted and said nothing.

S'mara allowed me to watch over her for a while

longer before I helped her sit up and fed her meat and the sweet gladvin roots. She tried to take the food from me to eat, and I snarled at her, holding out small pieces for her to take from my fingers. She did so with a look of amusement, leaning forward slightly to take the food from me as I offered it. I ate only when she was full and had settled back into the furs. I'd already put the cover back over the cave's entrance but moved it when S'mara needed to relieve herself. She let me help her up and didn't mind even when I refused to turn around. I stared at a spot over her head and into the distance, trying not to wonder when the Ghaal would send out more scouts.

Because they would.

The first group not returning would have confirmed all they needed to know—the human female was here with me. Killing them hadn't protected our location, but it certainly made me feel better.

My only consolation was the hours it would have taken for them to walk here, and we would have at least a day, if not a day and a half, before they assumed the group wouldn't be returning and sent out others with more weapons.

Back inside, with the cover on the cave secure, S'mara patted the furs next to her, and I lay down as invited. She immediately snuggled up next to me, curling her small body against mine and wrapping an arm over my chest, nuzzling her nose into my rib cage. I stilled, letting her get comfortable, and only looked down when she started giggling.

"Why are you laughing?"

S'mara placed her hand over her mouth, unsuccessfully covering her smile. "I'm sorry, it's just... you're so tense. It's like cuddling a statue."

"I didn't want to come on too strong and frighten you."

S'mara looked to be about to protest when her gaze traveled down my body, and she noticed my loincloth tented with my arousal. "Oh, Lanir, you don't frighten me anymore. I'm sorry."

My head whipped to the side. "What are you apologizing for?"

"Because..." she started, gesturing at my erect cock, "... you're aroused and... well..." Her cheeks flushed a pink, warm color in the light of the small fire. "I want to do things with you, but I'm.... inexperienced." She lifted a shoulder before adding, "And embarrassed. This is all new to me and would be new to me at home with another human, let alone... you. But I feel like I'm holding out on you or something."

I rolled to the side, realizing my mistake too late when my cock pressed against her warm stomach, and she released a squeak of surprise. I pretended not to notice the ache as she squirmed against me, creating only the slightest friction against my shaft, and stared into her eyes. "I will never make you do anything you don't want to do."

"I know that." Her cheeks flushed again. "Can I touch you?"

My back stiffened as I took in her words, and it was an effort not to grind against her warm body and release my cum against her. "Are you well enough?"

"Yes."

"Then yes."

With a small smile, she nodded, placing her hands on my chest and tracing her fingers around the lines of my muscles. I didn't take my gaze from her face, watching her changing expressions as she felt my body. Her skin looked so pale against mine—otherworldly. I almost chuckled at the thought until her hand traced down my stomach, and my breath hitched when she reached for the edge of my loincloth.

I needed to talk to S'mara about how we had to leave, but every time I tried to speak, the words were lost in a growl I had little control over. I shuddered, and when I smelled S'mara's arousal in the air, I snarled, gripping her lower back in my palm. My pheromones would be working overtime, releasing into the air and increasing the sensations she'd be experiencing. I couldn't stop them, and part of me didn't want to. I wanted her to find pleasure in touching me. I wanted to taste her sweet cunt, to feel the essence of what I could smell in the air directly on my tongue.

She fiddled with the ties and released my loincloth, pulling it to the side. I watched intently as she glanced down and gasped. Was my cock horrible to her? I was about to ask when she reached down and grabbed it tightly. With another growl, I thrust forward into her hand, unable to stop myself. S'mara touching my cock felt better than I had imagined, and I wanted more.

"Can I..." Her cheek flushed a deeper shade of pink, and I tore my gaze away from her hand around my cock long enough to meet her eyes. "Put my mouth on you?"

She ducked her head to my chest, blushing furiously as I shuddered under her touch. "You want to..." I swallowed, feeling as though I would come in her hand at the thought. "Use your mouth..."

"I've never done it before," she added quickly, and a territorial growl worked its way through my throat. *Good.* I wanted to say, *you're no one's to touch but mine.* "So, if it doesn't feel good, tell me, okay?"

I nodded, though I doubted she could do anything that *wouldn't* feel good. S'mara guided me to lay on my back, and I did, shifting backward so I could sit up halfway—I wanted to watch everything she was doing. With a shy smile, she peppered kisses down my stomach and over my thighs, taking the time to explore my body. She said I wasn't a monster to her, and with the way she was touching me, I had to believe her. She was too gentle and caring for this to be the motions of someone who found the being they were touching repulsive.

When she kissed the tip of my cock, I groaned, buckling up into her hand again. S'mara pulled her head away, surprised, and giggled when I apologized. "It's okay, just um… try to stay still."

Gripping the furs, I nodded again, and this time she opened her mouth and pulled the head of my cock past her lips. I groaned, digging my blunt claws into my palms, trying to remain still for her. She started bobbing her head up and down on the tip of my cock, and I could feel her tongue working against the sensitive skin underneath. Her hands moved up and down on my shaft in tandem with her mouth, and I imagined the only thing in this universe more exquisite than her mouth could only be sinking into her sweet cunt.

I knew I wouldn't last long, and my attempts to stop my hips from bucking into her mouth were failing. "S'mara…" I growled out. She hummed and sped up her movements. With a roar, I came and watched with wide eyes as S'mara didn't pull back but instead swallowed my cum as it pumped into her throat.

She moved her mouth off me, smiling, and

squeaked with surprise when I launched off the furs and grabbed her shoulders, plunging my tongue into her mouth. My musky scent was all over her tongue, and she groaned with me as I lifted her and laid her down where I had been. She wore the simple dress I'd made her, and when I flipped it up, I realized I'd not made her any pants. Snarling, I thought it was better this way—I could sneak glances at her glistening pink cunt all day.

"Can I taste you?" I asked, barely containing my growl. I was shaking with my need to taste her, but I promised her I would never touch without permission. S'mara's trust was more important than any desire I had.

"Yes," she said in a breathy whisper, and with a groan, I leaned forward, spreading her soft thighs with my hands and licking up her cunt, parting her pussy lips with my tongue. I wanted to dive my tongue inside but reminded myself she was a virgin. So instead, I teased her entrance with the tip of my tongue, pushing it in only slightly and back out again with small, gentle thrusts that had her writhing and grinding against my mouth.

"Here," she whispered, reaching down and touching herself. "My clit. Please. Lick it."

Her clit, a small pink nub at the top of her cunt, glistened with her juices, and when I ran my tongue over it, her hips bucked against my face.

Yes.

I wanted more of that reaction. I wanted her so needy for me that she ground against my face, chasing her release. I wanted S'mara to use me. I mumbled her name against her as I dived forward, sucking and licking at her clit. The noises she made only surged me on, and she wasn't shy now, leaning forward to grab my head and pull it between her welcoming thighs.

"Can I?" I ran a finger up and down through her wetness, and when I glanced up, S'mara was biting her lip, her hips still gyrating gently against where my mouth had been at the lost contact.

"Be gentle," she whispered, and I nodded, unable to form any words with her delicious taste coating my tongue. Of course, I could be gentle with her. It would take every ounce of strength I had to fight against my instincts and the desire to claim her as my mate right now.

When I pushed a finger against her entrance, her legs twitched and jolted. Still lapping my tongue gently against her sensitive clit, I watched her face. Her eyes were screwed shut, but she said nothing, so I pushed a little harder, and when I broke past the resistance of her cunt, she cried out.

I stopped, my finger buried inside her, the scent of her arousal increasing and washing over me, fueling my desire. "Are you okay, S'mara?" I grumbled out, desperate to maintain control.

She nodded frantically, her brows still furrowed.

When she opened her eyes, she held my eye contact, and her pupils were dilated with lust. "Keep going."

I kept it slow, dragging my finger in and out of her tight cunt as I wished to do with my cock, and continued to tongue at her clit. S'mara was close to coming, clenching so tight around my finger that movement was difficult. I wasn't going to stop, not until I felt her release flood my mouth.

When she came, S'mara cried out again, gripping my head with her fingers as her heels dug into my shoulders. I snarled against her, unable to stop until she sagged, energy drained from her body with the force of her release. Removing my finger from her was sweet agony, and I dipped it into my mouth, sucking her juices from my skin to prolong the joy of her taste. Just the scent of her release was enough for my cock to twitch again, hardening and ready to take her.

But not yet, not tonight.

I would wait for S'mara to come to me.

SAMARA

Lanir lay gently next to me, his movements tentative as I slumped back against the pile of furs and animal skins. My legs shook, and my toes curled. I'd *never* come that hard in my life.

And I'd never been closer to wanting to lose my virginity.

His finger had stretched me, but once the initial ache had eased, it had felt incredible, coupled with his tongue on me. I wanted more, but I didn't want to be greedy. Instead, I sighed with contentment and snuggled against Lanir's chest. It took a moment for him to relax against me, and when he finally draped an arm over my shoulder and held me close, I smiled against his skin.

"S'mara," Lanir grumbled, tilting his head to inhale against my hair.

I hummed my acknowledgment of his words, but my energy was draining, sleep wanting to take over as the day caught up with me. He made a grunting noise before continuing and fidgeted against me. Opening my eyes, I peered up at his troubled face. "What's wrong?"

"Tomorrow we must leave."

He said it quickly as though to soften the blow, and I'm not even sure why I was so shocked. Had I so quickly accepted this cave with this alien man as my new home? The idea of leaving it so soon filled me with unease, and my stomach churned with nerves. "Why?" I asked, unsuccessfully trying to hide the whine in my voice.

"It's not safe here. The Ghaal know you're here. When their scouts do not return, they'll send more."

I wanted to say that I trusted Lanir to protect me, but I bit my lip against the words. I didn't want him to be forced to fight off and kill others because of me. That was too much to ask. "Where will we go?"

"We'll keep moving. I can show you different parts of my home planet."

I curled my fingers against his chest, and he pulled me closer again. "For how long?"

"Some days, then we'll find my brother."

"Lanir," I said, placed my palm flat on his chest, and resisted the urge to smile. His expression was serious and strained with lines pulled tight at the corners of his lips. "How about instead of drip-feeding me information, you tell me what your plan is?"

"I will keep you safe."

I smiled. "Thank you, I know that. Please tell me your plan."

He tensed. "I don't know what to do." The admission seemed to pain him. "Ilk will know what to do."

I bit my lip, furrowing my brows as I tucked my head against his chest and thought. Lanir only wanted to protect me. He'd proved that more than once, and I trusted him with my life because he'd saved it. He was afraid because he didn't know what to do about the Ghaal. His brother, Ilk—he pronounced it with a strange click at the end I couldn't replicate when I whispered it to myself— would apparently know what to do. Or maybe they could work out something together.

"And the others?" I asked, looking up at his face again. "The other girls... we'll find them too?"

"Yes."

His jaw was taut, and I wondered if he was more worried about their safety than he was letting on. Frowning, I watched his expression. He'd told me his brothers would keep them safe, but how could he be sure?

I bit back the questions he seemed to have no answers for.

At least for now.

Lanir shifted against me. I woke slowly and pulled myself from the dream I'd been having. The details were fuzzy and slipped through my fingers every second as I woke—something about being chased, orange eyes, and unable to run when I needed to. I shuddered. Lanir froze halfway through sitting up and fell back against his elbow. Without a word, he pulled me against him, and I tucked my head next to his ribs and inhaled heavily.

Earthy, strong, masculine.

Opening my eyes a slit, I glanced at his loincloth. He was aroused again, and I sighed heavily. Lanir may look like a demon, but he'd shown more care and restraint than I could have imagined the beast he appeared to be would be capable of.

When I pulled away from him, Lanir stood, stretched his arms high, his fingertips scraped the cave's ceiling, and his loincloth tented with his erection. It was difficult not to stare, but if he noticed my attention, he didn't say anything, choosing to ignore it. I wanted to take him into my mouth again. I'd enjoyed going down on Lanir much more than I thought I would. There was something incredibly powerful about having a seven-foot alien trembling under my touch.

Before I could suggest it, he said, "We'll leave today."

"When?"

"As soon as we pack some supplies."

"Oh." I wanted to stay, and I couldn't even say why. But Lanir was right—this place was no longer safe. As I glanced up at him, moving around the cave and gathering things, the emotion built up behind my eyes and threatened to escape through an outpouring of tears. This was more than a cave— this was Lanir's *home.* A place he had welcomed me into without question and cared for me even when I fought him off. He'd kept me fed, cleaned, and comfortable. Safe from the winds at night, and even tried to teach me how to look after myself when we couldn't even talk to each other. His world had been flipped upside-down the second I landed on this planet, and now he was giving up the comfort of his home too.

Sniffing, I wiped the back of my hand under my nose. "I'm sorry," I whispered.

Lanir turned and tilted his head in question. "Why?"

"You have to leave your home because of me, and I'm sorry. You've been through so much since I got here, and it's all my fault. I just feel responsible." To hide my emotions, I stood and moved toward the corner where the water bags were to check if they were full enough. Lanir grabbed my arm as I passed, and when I didn't look at him, he snarled, touched my chin, and pinched harder than I imagined he intended to.

"You're important, S'mara. I must keep you safe."

"I just feel like I ruined your life," I muttered, staring into his bright green eyes as they flashed with anger or disappointment, I couldn't be sure. I deserved his anger for taking his life away the same as mine had been taken from me.

"I was living, but I had no life," Lanir said, his lip curled into a snarl before his entire body seemed to sink under the weight of his words. "Keeping you safe gives me meaning."

I kept staring at him. It was a lot to take in after knowing him for less than a week, but from what he'd told me, it made sense. He'd made it his duty to protect species kidnapped by the Ghaal, but somewhere along the way, I'd become more than a mission to him. The Ghaal wanted me and the girls specifically over any other species they'd abducted.

We were in incredibly real danger, and Lanir cared.

About *me.*

But there were things I was certain he was hiding from me, and it wasn't simply a matter of his not having gotten around to telling me yet. I'm sure he was *hiding* something. Details he didn't want me to know about this planet, himself, his past, our situation—any or all—I didn't know. Maybe this trip would be a good chance for me to pick his brain.

Maybe he'd finally open up to me. I was having feelings for him, feelings I couldn't deny yet didn't quite understand. But if I were going to lose my virginity to him, I wanted to know him, *all* of him.

After I relieved myself outside and had a quick wash, I followed Lanir's lead and packed food and weapons in a small skin bag. Lanir insisted on carrying the supplies, along with the water bags, and picked up his spear as we stood by the entrance to the cave.

"Ready to go?"

I looked at him, the red of his skin almost glowing in the early morning light as the sun hit the curves of his muscles. He still looked like a demon, but he no longer terrified me. I'd gotten more than used to him, and now I knew who he was beyond how he looked, I thought he was quite handsome. I'd always been an advocate for someone's personality having the ability to change how attractive they appeared. Not in a sense that it made literal changes to their physical appearance, but someone could be attractive until they opened their mouth and you found out they're a terrible person, then suddenly they weren't good-looking anymore. Likewise, someone could look average, different, or just not be the type to tickle your fancy, but if you got to know them and fell in love, suddenly they were the most attractive person in the world.

Unable to help the smile that quirked my lips, Lanir hesitantly returned the look, unsure what I was thinking. I certainly held a great deal of affection for Lanir, but I don't think I was *in love* with him.

Yet.

When I held out my hand, he looked at it for a beat before curling his large fingers around mine, and we began making our way down the side of the mountain and away from the ocean.

Away from the Ghaal.

"Where will we go?" I asked.

Lanir scanned the horizon, keeping his gaze fixed in the distance before he glanced down at me. "Toward the forest. We'll keep moving, not spending more than a night or two in one place. After a few days, we'll find my brother and figure out what to do about your friends."

I nodded but couldn't help the disappointment settling in my chest. "We're not going to find my friends now?"

Lanir gripped my hand as I slipped on a smooth part of the rock. "We need to lose the Ghaal first.

When they come here and find we are gone, they will search. Their tracking technology is outdated and breaking down. When they can't find us within a few days, they'll return to their colony to regroup. Then it will be safer for us to find Ilk."

Safer but not *safe.* A shudder ran down my spine. "Lanir?" I whispered, and he grunted in response as he grabbed my waist and lifted me gracefully over a particularly jagged part of the rocks. "I have three questions this time." A low chuckle rumbled through his chest at that, but he still said nothing, so I continued, "Can I have a spear?"

He offered me a sideways glance as we walked. "What for?"

"So you can teach me to hunt." His lips tightened into a thin line, most likely thinking about the last time we tried to do that, so I added, "I want to learn, I do. It won't be easy for me, but if you're patient, I'll get used to it." I swallowed against the uncertainty rising in my throat—the memory of the small fluffy animal Lanir had killed in front of me and my immediate reaction of crying. I was trying to convince myself as much as him. "I don't want you to have to look after me all the time. I want to help."

His grip on my hand increased again before releasing a nervous twitch. "You wish to look after yourself?"

I squeezed his hand back. "I wish to *learn.* I'm not leaving you, Lanir."

He grunted, but I saw the corner of his mouth twitch. "What's question two?"

"If we're leaving the mountains and you're adaptive, won't your appearance change?"

Lanir shook his head. "It's not an instant change, this level of adaption..." he shifted his fingers to indicate his body, "... takes time. I won't change overnight. Were you..." when he looked at me, his large brow was furrowed. "Were you hoping I would?"

"No, just curious."

"You're curious about a lot of things."

I laughed at that, drawing another chuckle from Lanir as I did. "I'm on an alien planet... forgive me if I have questions."

"What's your last question?"

"My last question *for now.*" Another chuckle, and I loved I could make him happy. "What did the Ghaal say to you in his language?"

Lanir stiffened, and immediately, guilt welled in my chest for asking and bringing up a moment Lanir clearly wasn't proud of, but I had to know. I suspected this was the information he was withholding from me. The Ghaal had treated him badly, but there was more to it, a lot more he wasn't telling me, and I was unsure if it was to protect me from the horrors of the truth or protect himself from having to relive it.

"S'mara..." his tone held a warning, and when I

stumbled again, Lanir grunted and scooped an arm around my waist, steadying me as we finished the final and steepest descent from the mountain.

"I'm sorry. It's just… it must have been something bad, right? You were angry before, but after whatever he hissed out, you were…"

I didn't need to tell Lanir what he was because he already knew.

Animal.

Beast.

Deadly.

He didn't want to tell me. That much was apparent by his jaw clenching and how he paid extremely close attention to where we stepped, assessing every move when he would usually glide across this terrain as though he were part of it. I was torn between wanting to know and *not* wanting to know.

"He threatened you," he responded, and I debated internally whether to ask for more details. In the end, curiosity won out.

"Threatened how?"

"S'mara, please…"

Lanir had mentioned the Ghaal was cruel, and their intention was to breed us. What could be worse than using us as a breeding machine, implanting us with sperm to…

"Oh…" I whispered, looking down. "He threatened to…" I couldn't get the word *rape* out as

though saying it would make it too real. I had taken in everything Lanir had told me about the Ghaal, but in that moment, even more than when they came for me, the crushing reality of the danger I was in settled in my stomach.

"Yes." Lanir's teeth clenched, and he forced the word out, adding additional strange syllables as though, in his anger, he had reverted to his native language. "I will protect you."

He squeezed my hand again. Lanir had told me that before—*I will protect you*—and repeatedly, he'd proven it. So, I squeezed his hand back and pulled him to a stop long enough to lift myself onto my toes and kiss his cheek.

"I know you will."

CHAPTER 17

SAMARA

We walked all day, skirting around the woodlands with the sandy ground where those horrible little eylak things lived, and made our way through fields of yellowing fluffy grasses that brushed pleasantly against my shins. Occasionally, we'd stop and pull a handful of gladvin berries up by the roots, shaking off the rich soil and popping them in our mouths, savoring the sweet juice. Lanir said there wasn't much nutritional value in them, but they were a treat and soothed my thirst when water wasn't enough.

As far as I knew, there was no chocolate on this planet, so the root berries would have to do.

The sun lowered, and Lanir led me through another patch of grass to a rocky outcrop where we would camp for the night after hunting. Bending, I grabbed another handful of berries and shouted, "Open your mouth."

Lanir turned, his head tilted at me as his brow furrowed slightly.

I held up one of the berries and repeated, "Open your mouth." Lanir did slowly and with much confusion. As soon as he had, I tossed the berry and laughed when it landed on his exposed tongue. "Bull's-eye!" I cried, giggling at his confusion. Lanir bit down on the berry, his brow still furrowed. When I said, "Again," he obeyed, standing still with his mouth agape and watched me take a few hurried steps backward.

This time, I missed, and the berry bounced off his forehead. When I shrieked with laughter, Lanir chuckled. That deep rumbling sound sent the best kind of shivers down my spine. "You are strange, S'mara."

"Oh, come on, I'm just playing with you. Didn't you ever play?"

Lanir shook his head but opened his mouth obediently as I held another berry ready. Of course, he didn't play—he didn't have a childhood as he was created in a lab. It was difficult sometimes to remember that. Technology on Earth wasn't even close to simply creating a fully-grown intelligent being capable of reproducing. I wondered what it was like to wake up one day, fully conscious. I would have to ask him and mentally added it to my ever-growing list of questions.

This time, I made the shot into his mouth. Lanir even stretched up on his toes and leaned to catch it when my aim was off.

"Now you throw one to me," I said, opening my mouth and pointing just in case it wasn't obvious by now how to play this silly game.

Lanir looked uncertain and took a few steps toward me, tossing the berry in a gentle underarm toss so it arced upward but landed on my shoulder. A few more hits and misses, and he gained a bit of confidence—the berries weren't going to hurt me—and for a while, we ran around in circles, tossing them at each other and laughing.

When I missed one, catching it with the edge of my teeth and biting to save the shot, the berry burst and splashed my face and neck with the oily juice. I laughed, wiping my eyes, and when I opened them, Lanir was at my side, looking down at me with a darkened expression. Without a word, he took my hands, moved them away from my face, and leaned forward, dragging his tongue up my neck and over my cheek, following the trail of the sweet juice to the edge of my lips. I shuddered but didn't move or say anything, unwilling to break the trance he was under or the spell he was casting over me with his featherlight touches and caresses.

Lanir did it again, his tongue coming up the front of my throat as I obediently tilted my head back to give him access. When a growl rumbled through his throat, and he dipped his tongue lower toward my breasts, I moaned on instinct, arching my back.

He pulled away, released my hands, and took a few hurried steps backward.

"S'mara..." Lanir shook his head, rested a palm against his forehead, and closed his eyes. His scent washed over me as a gust of wind moved past us, lifting my tunic and bringing with it the wonderful smell of him. That masculine scent was back and stronger—his pheromones, designed to increase arousal.

It was working.

I moved toward him, dropping the remaining berries, forgotten and unimportant, and reached out to him. Lanir took another step back, "I didn't mean to—"

"Stop."

He did. He stopped moving away from me, stopped talking, and stopped dead in his tracks, all at my command. Lanir eyed me as I closed the gap between us. His chest rose and fell heavily with every arduous breath, his loincloth once again tented with his arousal, fluttering in the breeze and making my breath catch as I realized I wanted so desperately for it to shift so I could see his cock again. Placing my hands on his chest, I traced the lines of his muscles with my fingertips, pressing harder when he jerked as though he was going to pull away.

"S'mara..." his voice was a warning, telling me to stay away, to stop because he couldn't stop himself.

He still didn't realize I wanted this and him.

Shyness overcame me as the words were on the tip of my tongue, and with a small smile, I glanced at the ground, chuckling at the difference in size between our feet. "Lanir," I whispered. He stiffened under my touch, his hands coming up and stopping short of touching me, hesitating before he placed them gently on my waist. "I'd like to have sex with you."

I flinched at my words, cringing at how awkward I sounded, but I didn't know what else to say. I had no clue about how to seduce someone or tell them my thoughts and intentions in any way other than simply telling them the truth. Was there a courting practice I should be doing? From this planet or Earth? I was equally clueless as to both. When Lanir didn't answer, I finally found the nerve to drag my gaze, admiring his body on the way up, to rest on his eyes to find his gaze dark with lust and arousal.

"I don't want to hurt you," he grumbled, his fingers flexing on my waist.

I rubbed my upper arm and bit my lip. I was indecisive—I just didn't know how to tell him what I wanted to say, except to come right out and say it.

"I know it will hurt." His eyes widened at my confession, and I looked away again, returning his gaze only when he brought his hand to my chin and forced me to look at him. "It's my first time... it would hurt with anyone."

He growled, his lip lifting into a snarl as though the mere idea of me with someone else had him raging. I shuddered again—I liked that—he was so possessive and protective in the best possible way. He looked after me without making me feel like I was a burden. The only one who felt I wasn't worthy in this thing between us was *me*.

To him, I gave his life meaning.

It floored me.

"I know you'll be as gentle as possible, but I want this, Lanir." I bit my lip again. "I want *you.*"

He was trembling, and it was strange to see someone so large shake like that. But it wasn't fear. He was fighting for control, but an almost constant growl made itself known as his hands tightened on my waist, one hand sliding back over my ass to bring me closer to him.

"Are you sure?"

His tone was husky, reaching every part inside me and almost making me gasp simply at the sound of his voice. Reaching down, I finally flicked his loincloth out of the way and cupped his heavy balls in one hand, gripping his shaft in the other and drawing an agonized hiss from him. "I'm sure."

His arms surrounded me, scooping me next to his body as he straightened, spun, and bolted toward the rocky area we were to camp in. I giggled, wrapping my arms around his body and sighing as I pressed my cheek to his chest, jolting with every one of his large steps. His growls had become snarls when he stopped, and his heart thumped loudly against where I rested my ear.

Lanir lowered me to the ground, choosing a spot where the moss was spongy and thick on the rocks, and held his hand behind my head until I was comfortable, his brow furrowed as he was torn between concern and arousal. When I sat up, he tried to make me lay again, and I laughed, shifting his hands away so I could reach the bottom of my tunic, holding it, ready to pull over my head. My confidence waivered for a moment, and my cheeks flushed warm at Lanir's intense stare, kneeling at my feet and watching my hands, waiting patiently.

He was such a good man.

Good *alien,* good *Synth,* whatever he liked to be called.

With a deep breath, I pulled the tunic over my head, and Lanir's eyes flashed with lust, tracing every inch of my body with such intensity I could almost feel the touch against my skin.

"Lie down, S'mara," he rumbled out, his gaze never stopping its tour of my body as I rolled up my tunic in a makeshift pillow and lay back. "Get comfortable, my mate, so I can taste your cunt."

I shuddered, relaxing into his touch as he spread my legs with his large hands, and I looked down to watch as he lowered himself between my legs and inhaled deeply. On instinct, I tried to bring my legs together, embarrassed and concerned I might smell. But Lanir snarled and pushed my thighs open farther, completely exposing me to him. Lifting a finger, he pressed my clit, rubbing in small circles that had my hips lifting toward his touch and gyrating. I already felt the flush of wetness between my legs and laid back, gripping the moss under my fingers as he tongued at my pussy's entrance.

I moaned as he penetrated me with his thick tongue, the muscle moving inside me and swirling around, opening me up as his finger kept working my clit. His scent surrounded me, sucking me into a world where nothing existed but his touch, and even the slight scratch of the moss against my back was forgotten in the pleasure. My peak built quickly, and I gripped Lanir's head as he plunged his tongue into me, pumping it in and out and pushing harder with his finger, forcing me to climax. When I came, he reached up and pressed his palm over my mouth to muffle my scream as he continued to work me through my peak until I writhed under his touch.

Lanir crawled over me, forcing my thighs to stay apart to accommodate the size of him between them. His cock sat heavily against my stomach, streaking wet precum over my skin as he thrust gently against me. "Don't scream, S'mara. We aren't secure in my cave tonight."

Glancing around, I bit my lip, my thighs clenching around his hips. "Are we safe?"

"You're always safe with me, my mate." I looked up at him and held onto his arms as he rested his palms on either side of my head. "But no screaming." His lip lifted into a smirk, and I smiled at him. Lanir's expression turned serious as he reached down to grab his cock, guiding it toward my waiting pussy. "Are you sure, S'mara? I'll never pressure you."

"I know you won't." I sighed at his comforting weight against me and ran my hands up his arms and over his shoulders. This entire situation seemed so surreal and hyperreal at the same time. I was sensitive to every touch and brush of his chest against mine as he breathed, the rub of his waist between my thighs, and most of all, the head of his cock poised at my pussy's entrance. "I want this, please."

"I will go slow."

I nodded as he pushed forward. I cried out and bit my hand as the head of his cock penetrated me.

There was pain, a sharp prick followed by an uncomfortable stretch as my body tried to accommodate him. I whined and shifted my hips from side to side as I tried to ease the pressure, opening my legs wider and doing anything to take away the discomfort.

The growl in his chest was back, and I looked at Lanir's face to see his eyes were closed, his jaw taut as he grit his teeth. He was trying too hard not to hurt me, and I wanted this to be good for him. I didn't want to get caught up in the pain. So, I took a few deep breaths and tried to force my body to relax, reaching down to brush my clit.

When Lanir felt my hand between us, he snarled, slapping my hand away gently and sucking on his finger before rubbing it against my clit. When I moaned, he rocked his hips forward, and I cried out again, then whimpered as he penetrated me another few inches. He continued rocking gently, keeping a steady and light touch on my clit, enough to bring pleasure and relax my body so he could fit his cock inside me.

Tears I couldn't help leaked from my eyes when he was fully seated inside me after one final, harsh thrust, my body fighting against the intrusion. He removed his hand from between us long enough to wipe the tears from my cheeks. "Are you okay? We can stop."

"No, no. Please don't stop. I want this."

Lanir nodded but didn't look convinced and waited a beat before returning his fingers to my clit. His ministrations became harder and more urgent, but he wasn't thrusting. "Maybe it'll help if you come around my cock." He growled.

I moaned at his words, shuddered again, and felt another flush of warmth as I got wetter. Lanir felt it too, groaning, and he rubbed my clit in circles, determined to bring me to another climax. My legs began to tremble as I got close, and Lanir muttered, "That's it... I can feel your cunt squeezing around me. I want to make you come."

Gasping, I arched my back. "Keep talking," I panted out.

Lanir's eyebrow twitched before his expression darkened. "I need you to come, S'mara, so I can fuck into you properly, so I can feel you stretch around me and make you come again and again as I thrust hard into you. I'm going to hold your pretty thighs apart and watch my cock sink deep into your virgin cunt. Your cunt was made for me, only for me, my mate."

With a shudder, I bit my hand again, crying out as I came around his cock, harder than I had before. The pleasure of his touch combined with the stretch was almost too much, and his words made me want everything he said more than I'd wanted anything physical before. I don't think I'd ever be able to come again without his cock inside me. There wasn't any other way it would be as satisfying.

As I came down, the pleasure lingered longer, my pussy clenching around Lanir's thickness seated deep inside me. Every clench and twitch sent another pulse of pleasure through me. Lanir shifted, pulling out slowly and back in with a gentle motion, and I moaned. The pressure was still there, feeling like I couldn't stretch my legs wide enough to ease it. But every drag of him inside me sent another jolt of pleasure through me, and I gripped Lanir's forearms, held his eye contact, and nodded.

I offered him a small smile. "Fuck me, Lanir."

With a groan, he thrust again, a bit harder than before, and involuntarily, I clenched, trying to keep him inside me rather than trying to push him out. He looked at me for reassurance, and when I nodded, he did it again, thrusting a bit harder and faster each time, his control waning with every movement. My body responded, making me wetter around him, and I bit my lip against the onslaught of moans that threatened to surface. How was I supposed to keep quiet? It felt impossibly good, and I ran my hands up Lanir's arms and over his shoulders, pulling him down on top of me while his hips pistoned, fucking me against the mossy ground.

The growl in his chest was louder, more insistent, and vibrated against me as he bore down on top of me, trapping me between him and the ground. I shuddered around him, and when he moved to his knees, holding my thighs open and watching his cock penetrate me exactly as he said he would, we moaned together.

I jerked when he reached down to touch my clit after resting my leg against his shoulder, and he smirked, his eyes flashing dangerously and looking all the more the demon I first thought he was. I didn't think I had the strength left for another release, but his motions were insistent, rubbing in small circles and building the pressure, tightening the coil until I was ready to snap.

"Lanir!" I gasped out, lurched forward to grab him, and settled for placing my hands against his knees as he drove into me, my hips lifted from the ground to meet his thrusts.

When I came, I threw my head back and arched off the ground, pressing a palm over my mouth to try to stop the sound of my climax. Lanir returned to gripping my thighs, lifting me higher and fucking harder into me, his release followed with a snarl as he spilled his cum inside me. The warmth of it flooded me, and when he slowly pulled out, I whimpered, feeling the wetness dripping down my thighs.

Lanir lay on top of me. He clasped his hands together over my head and rested his forearms on the ground, nipping and licking at my neck and ear, the growls from his chest joined by his snarls as we shuddered together in the aftermath of pleasure.

"My mate," Lanir whispered, the words edged with a growl.

I felt his cock twitch against me and draped my arms around him, tracing the lines of the muscles on his back with my fingers. "Yours."

LANIR

S'mara had welcomed me between her thighs last night, and after I was forced to leave our camp to hunt, leaving her side for only as long as was necessary, we spent the rest of the night pressed against each other. I was the only protection S'mara had out here from the strong winds that came every night. I'd chosen the rocky outcrop specifically so she could sleep between the rocks and me, as guarded as she could be. With her belly full of meat and fruit and her womb full of my seed, S'mara slept peacefully, her small hands clutched at my chest whenever I shifted as she slept. I breathed in her scent and lingering arousal, my cock hard against her. With only the slightest shift, I could sink into her again, lift one of her smooth thighs over my hip and penetrate her hot cunt, filling her with my seed again.

But she needed sleep, and I could rest knowing she had let me claim her as her first and only.

She woke slowly, and I was in no rush to move her, waiting until she rubbed her eyes and blinked before looking up at me. A part of me waited for her to shove me away, tell me it was a mistake to let me fuck her, and she no longer wished to be near me. But instead, she smiled, lifted herself onto an elbow, and planted a gentle kiss against my lips.

"Good morning," she said.

I grunted. She shifted against my cock when she moved, and S'mara looked down between us, giggling when she noticed my arousal. She reached down and grabbed my shaft, and I thrust into her hand before she languidly dragged her fingers up my length and snatched her hand away when I growled.

"Sorry," she muttered, her cheeks flushing. "I like touching it."

"You can touch my cock whenever you want to, S'mara."

She nodded, her cheeks still flamed with a pink tinge, and I grabbed her, burying my face next to her neck and inhaling deeply. Squirming and giggling, she pulled away. "Shouldn't we get going?"

We needed to keep moving, but I didn't want to. I wanted to take S'mara back to my cave or find a new one and fuck her every moment of the day. I was sure she'd open up to me easier next time and easier again the time after that. Soon, I'd be able to slide into her waiting cunt, but she'd always grip me so deliciously tight.

So small.

So delicate.

Made for my cock.

Snarling, I nodded and stretched my arms as S'mara took a drink. We loaded up our supplies, finished off the gladvin roots we had picked the day before, and set off toward the woodlands. They spanned far, and one of my brothers, Eldich, lived deep in them. I doubted we would come across him, and I was hesitant to purposefully seek him out. He was always the secluded type, even before we split. Ilk would have a better idea of what to do and be more adept at developing a plan. Eldich could be influenced, and I was not the type he should be around alone.

Besides, I wanted to keep S'mara to myself, at least for a little longer.

We would skirt the edge of the woodlands, keeping to the fields where the ground was more even and an easier walk for S'mara. We'd follow the fields to the edge of the smaller hills farther inland and take a large loop that would lead us back to where Ilk resided.

S'mara kept asking me if we could find her friends, and each time, I ended the conversation by telling her my brothers would have found them. I could only hope I wasn't unknowingly lying to her, and my gut twisted at the idea I was giving her false hope. My brothers would have made every effort to get to the units if they were in our territory. But as history had proven, sometimes we weren't fast enough.

If my brothers reached the units before the Ghaal and saw the human women step out, would they understand how important they were? I hoped so. We had already split to different parts of the continent by the time Ilk and I found the human female who had been cut up, the remnants of the last lot of humans the Ghaal had managed to have abducted. Vitri, who resided in the forest, may have been aware. Sahcor in the oceans? He was almost as much of a loner as Eldich was. I wasn't much for talking, but I missed living with my brothers. My past was splattered with the blood of the things I had done to protect myself and them, and being apart from them was hard.

But it was for the best. If together, we'd be unable to resist changing genders to breed with each other. Our bodies adapted against our will, and we were designed to breed. Besides the changes the environment had on our beings, alone together and half of us, or more, would end up as females. We remained male in the Ghaal's lab through sheer determination, but more than once, I felt my body attempting to change. I'd wake some mornings with a slenderer waist, slight breasts, and wider thighs. I'd rage until I brought it under control.

But it wouldn't work forever.

I believe the Ghaal noticed I was the first to show signs of changing gender, and this is why I was singled out as the weakest link—the one they would inflict punishment on to try to bend us to their will.

They treated me like a monster, and I became one.

Gritting my teeth, I huffed out a fast breath through my nose. S'mara glanced up at me as we walked, offering me a small but confused smile and squeezed my hand. She would ask me questions about the planet as we walked, about plant and animal species, and I would do my best to answer. But I could see it in her eyes that she had more questions.

She wanted to know more about me, my past, and how I came to be who I am.

Would she hate me for the things I had done?

Or could she forgive me as she had when I'd killed those Ghaal to protect her?

I would eventually have to tell her about the female Ilk and I found, her body broken and destroyed. S'mara deserved to know she and her friends weren't the first humans to be taken by the Ghaal. The first lot hadn't survived if the way we found the body was anything to go by. The Ghaal, in their excitement at having found a match, had cut them up to confirm the pregnancy when they could no longer trust their instruments. Now they knew the humans were compatible. They would keep them caged until they showed signs of pregnancy and gave birth and then use them over and over again.

Shaking my head, I shouldn't think of such things. It was difficult to maintain my composure when I did. All I could think of was ending the Ghaal with violence, the same violence Ilk never approved of.

Maybe if he came across one of the human females, he would remember in as much vivid detail as I did, and he would realize that perhaps it was time to take action, and we were fools to hope for a peaceful solution for this long. The longer the gaps between unit drops, the more I hoped each would be the last.

But I knew better—they would never stop.

They didn't deserve to live.

S'mara and her friends would be the last. They were on the planet now, and the Ghaal wouldn't give up trying to find them, never stopping until they had them all together.

Ilk would be forced to see my view. We should've put a stop to this years ago.

Glancing down at S'mara, I squeezed her hand, and she looked away from the flowers she'd been admiring and smiled at me, her eyes bright with wonder at the plants that blossomed with flowers bigger than her.

However, if we had wiped out the Ghaal, S'mara would never have been brought to me.

It was a selfish thought, but one I couldn't help having because she was mine now, and I hers.

After we took a break, the sun at its peak in the sky above us, S'mara watched me carefully when we started walking again. Every time I glanced at her, she was watching me. Even if I pointed out things along the way, she would still return her gaze to me.

"Are you okay, Lanir?" she eventually asked in a small voice as though preparing herself for a negative reaction from me. "You seem distracted."

"I have a lot of things on my mind."

"About me? And why I'm here?"

Snarling, my fangs were exposed as I lifted my top lip in the rush of anger that flooded me, and every thought of the threats made against S'mara came forward. I wouldn't lie to her, but I also couldn't bring myself to openly tell her the truth.

My S'mara was brave, facing this planet as though it were an adventure, even when her features were strained under the stress of her situation.

She dropped her gaze from me then and looked at her feet. "Are you ever going to tell me what you know about why I'm here?"

"I've told you the Ghaal's intentions."

"There's more though, isn't there? There's something you're not telling me. I can feel it."

When I didn't respond and instead ground my teeth together and clamped my jaw, S'mara nodded sadly and slowly withdrew her hand from mine. I wanted to shout she was safer this way and better off not knowing the fate of those who came before her. But the trust we'd built since I found her was being eroded by what I *wasn't* telling her.

With a roar, I punched a nearby tree, the truck cracking and bending under the impact. S'mara squealed and jumped, clasping her hands over her mouth as her eyes darted between the tree I had broken and me. There was no way around it. S'mara wasn't a pet I could keep safe and uninformed. I needed her to trust me, and she needed to know the truth.

"Sit," I demanded, pointing at the ground.

S'mara looked at me for a moment longer before she lowered her hands from her face, sank into the thick yellow grass, and crossed her legs. She looked even smaller, dwarfed, and partially hidden by the grasses as I stood over her, and I ran my hand down my face before crouching next to her, staring intently at her face. After a few moments, S'mara leaned back from the intensity of my expression, and I snorted in frustration again.

"Lanir, you can tell me. I can handle it," she said, reaching out as if to take my hand but brushing her fingers down my arm instead.

My voice was gruff. "She had the same hair color as you."

S'mara's eyes widened.

Whatever she expected me to say, it wasn't that. I doubted myself again, not only about what I was telling her but *how.* I couldn't simply talk about the female as if she were just an object in a story. This was her story, and it was a sad one because before I even knew she existed, she was already dead, having suffered at the hands of the Ghaal.

I continued, "My brother, Ilk, and I found her when a Ghaal was trying to dispose of her body. We didn't know her name, so we named her Laloisa. It seemed wrong to bury her without a name."

S'mara's eyes were shining with unshed tears, her hand delicately over her mouth, not quite covering the trembling of her lip. The feel of the soil on my fingers as I dug the grave was so strong in my memory that I almost expected to look down and see my hands covered in dirt. Snarling again, I shook my head clear of the memories. I needed to be clearer for S'mara. She needed to understand why I was so desperate to keep her safe.

Why I'd held her in my cave when she wanted to leave.

Why I'd killed for her.

"You and your friends are not the first humans to be on this planet." S'mara opened her mouth to ask a question but stopped when my shoulders tensed. If I was going to tell her of Laloisa, I needed to get the words out quickly, hoping it would make them less painful. "The Ghaal had humans before you, six of them. They always work in sixes. When it turned out the human females were compatible for breeding, in their haste to confirm the pregnancies, they killed the females, cutting and slicing them up. Some of the deaths would have been for experiments, but the Ghaal needed more humans after that. They had a deal with the Moeks to find more females, but the longer the deal went on, the more species the Moeks brought in lieu of humans the more payment they got. The Ghaal continued to test the species delivered for compatibility, knowing all along they were waiting for more humans. Then there was you..." I met her eyes, trying to keep my scowl hidden in case she misread it. My feelings of hostility weren't for her. "And your friends—"

"But there's only four of us. I thought you said they always worked in sixes."

"The Ghaal are beyond desperate now. It's been several generations since the war, and their numbers are few. If four is all the Moeks offered, they would take the four of you, superstitions be damned."

"And Laloisa?" she asked.

"My brother and I found her cut up and dead." I shuddered. "She would have been so beautiful... before. I could tell. When I saw you, I knew I couldn't let you out of my sight. I didn't realize until I saw you that I had fallen in love with Laloisa then and there. I saw her purity and innocence and how she suffered like I had at the hands of the Ghaal. In my mind, you were her, and she was you. Then you were so pure yourself, everything I was created to protect and love. You're my mate, my second chance, when I was too late to save her." I sighed heavily, pulling up a handful of grass and popping one of the gladvin root berries in my mouth, just for something to do. The sweet juices tasted sour on my tongue. "But I was selfish with you." I looked at S'mara, pleading without words for her forgiveness. "There are bigger things at play here, and part of me wanted, and still wants, to keep you to myself."

"And my friends?" Her voice was small and shook with emotion.

"We will find Ilk, then find them. I was telling you the truth. We must keep moving like this to shake the Ghaal from our trail."

She nodded. "I'm sorry, Lanir."

My head shot up, and my brows furrowed. What was she apologizing for? "I'm the one who should be apologizing. It's a difficult memory to relive. My brothers and I have always tried to save all the abducted species, and we can't always do it. But Laloisa's death hit harder than the others. It's selfish of me to feel that way and not to have told you about her."

"I feel like I know her." S'mara pressed a small hand to her chest over her heart.

"Me too."

"And the others?" When I simply looked at her, her eyebrows flickered upward, urging me for information. "The other human females who were taken with Laloisa... the five others? Did you find their bodies too?"

I shook my head. "No. Only Laloisa."

"So..." her brow furrowed before she looked at me, her eyes sparking with fear and excitement. "They could still be in the Ghaal colony. We could rescue them!"

"No. The Ghaal told us their experiments cost them the females' lives. That's why you and your friends were taken."

Her shoulders slumped. "Oh."

"I'm sorry, S'mara."

"Lanir..." She studied my face. "What did the Ghaal do to you?"

Somehow, she'd hit right on the one nerve I'd been protecting so hard, and I physically flinched, turning away from her concerned expression at my reaction. "I will tell you. Just not today."

S'mara nodded and reached out to intertwine her fingers with mine.

The trust was back.

She was my mate again.

CHAPTER 19

SAMARA

My curiosity and wonder at the strange plants and animals we'd encountered waned as the day went on, and exhaustion took hold. Easily ninety percent of the species we'd spotted were introduced from other planets, including the plants. Abducted species came here with seeds in their fur, hair, or digestive systems, and the plants had taken over the natives. Most of the native animals were wiped out or pushed to extinction by the Ghaal's wars with their use of chemical warfare, and most of the animal species here now were thanks to the intergalactic trade to help replenish the planet's food supplies. The planet had a rich atmosphere and soil, and species thrived. Now, the environment was a mishmash of species from across the galaxies learning to live here. Lanir told me there weren't many predators, and most of the abducted species that they'd successfully steered away from the Ghaal colony lived in seclusion and kept to themselves.

But some things were dangerous, and he told me I should never venture off alone.

I remembered the eylaks and how they had taken down Lanir with the smallest stab of venom into his heel, and I shuddered. I wouldn't be going off alone any time soon.

We were moving, and Lanir had stressed how important this was. He and his brothers knew where each other was, and he'd expressed his concern Ilk would come looking for him and find his cave empty. But my safety was more important, and we would get back to Ilk in due time.

I was curious to meet his family.

They weren't really related—each assembled from a random assortment of Ghaal and created DNA designed to breed with each other. They called each other brothers to cement the bond created when they suffered together in the lab. Although what that suffering meant, Lanir had yet to tell me. I didn't want to push him. The way his shoulders tensed and his teeth ground together, his eyes darkened with horrific memories that haunted him. I didn't want to be the one to bring that all to the surface. But I wanted to know all about him, even the things he kept hidden in the shadows.

Lanir had already shared with me about the human he'd found before me, already dead. I think he blamed himself for being unable to save her, like it was somehow his fault. I didn't know what to say but hoped my comforting him was enough for him to know I didn't blame him, and he shouldn't blame himself either.

I was even keener to meet Ilk. I was holding onto the hope he had found another one of the girls so strongly I thought it might burst and evaporate. I wanted her to be safe in a cave too, learning to hunt, forage, and the dangers of this planet with a big alien of her own to look after and protect her.

Hopefully, they all were safe.

My stomach rumbled loudly, and Lanir glanced down at me. "We'll hunt."

I nodded and opened my mouth to offer to help, lost my nerve, and looked at my feet instead. Again, the feeling of uselessness washed over me, and I hated it. I wanted to be stronger, able to take charge and work *with* Lanir, rather than him having to baby me.

"Let me show you something," Lanir grumbled, and I looked up to find him watching my face, studying the transition of expressions I'm sure had been on display. I never was much good at keeping a poker face. "Grab your knife."

I hesitated, my hand hovering over where I had it slung by my waist with a strap over my opposite shoulder. Lanir's lip lifted into a smirk, and he nodded, gesturing for me to take it. I wrapped my hand around the leather-bound handle of the bone blade and held it at the ready. Lanir let go of my hand and moved toward the edge of the woodlands. Nervously, I watched my feet, but the soil was different here. It wasn't the loose, dappled sand of the woodlands closer to the mountain and ocean, but a deeper and richer brown with a thick covering of deep green moss in most places. Breathing a sigh of relief, I followed as Lanir stalked into the woods. The trees looked similar to the ones around Lanir's cave home, the ones he had stripped the rubbery bark off for a snack and to start fires. But as the days passed, the scenery had changed, and I marveled at how every inch of this place seemed to be a constantly changing wonder of different plants and ecosystems.

The sun was shining clearly through the treetops, thin branches spread far, allowing lots of light to the moss below. Looking up, thick clouds were coming in from the ocean, and I glanced nervously at Lanir. Was it going to rain? And we'd be stuck sleeping outside?

An image of dancing naked in the rain with an incredibly confused Lanir watching formed in my mind, and I giggled. He turned to look at me, an eyebrow arched, and I waved a hand dismissively. *Not important enough to talk about.*

Besides, maybe I'd act it out later just to see how confused I could make him.

Sighing, I smiled, thankful for my mind bringing me back on track to focus on the smaller things, the stop-and-smell-the-flowers type moments that I should be thinking about—an ability I had that had been put to the extreme test these past few weeks, but was glad I still had it.

Glass half full and all of that.

Lanir stopped by a larger, almost mustardy yellow tree with a thick trunk I don't think even Lanir could reach around entirely.

"Hand me your knife," he whispered. I did so without question and kept quiet. I didn't like we were whispering, but I reminded myself Lanir would never put me in danger. With another smirk, he said, "You're going to get us food tonight. You can cook for me."

I opened my mouth to question him and yelped when he plunged the knife into the side of the tree, pulling downward and opening a large gaping hole in the side.

The tree seemed to change color, and I held back a horrified scream when I realized it was a flood of small insects funneling out of the cut Lanir had made. With speed, he stabbed and dropped them to the ground, one stab in the back of their heads and flicked them from his knife until a small pile formed at his feet. As quickly as the insects had appeared, they disappeared, moving into the tree's foliage until the woodlands were silent again.

Lanir picked up one of the insects and handed it to me. I cringed, biting back my retort, and held out my hand to take it from him.

Closer, I realized it wasn't an insect.

More like a rat with armor.

Great.

Lanir held out the knife. "Your turn."

I glanced between his face, the knife, and the creature in my hand. They were around the size of my palm, and I imagined we'd need a lot to feed Lanir and me. Despite the smirk on his face, I think he was trying to ease me into this.

I'd have to learn to hunt eventually, right?

"Okay," I said, nodding my head once, trying to convince myself as much as I could that I was ready. "Let's do this."

Lanir pointed casually to another tree behind me, and I spun, gripping the knife between both hands before rethinking and holding it in my right hand and positioning it so I could stab downward.

"Once you cut the tree, you'll have seconds to get as many as possible."

Nodding, I bit my lip and took a few deep breaths. This was for survival, and they were quick kills—humane. I told myself everything I needed to keep me hyped up and reminded this wasn't like any situation I'd been in before.

This was my new life.

Biting my lip harder to stop it from trembling, I swung my arm and sliced into the tree. It was like cutting into a mattress, a thin, flexible outside skin that opened up to a spongy interior. The armored rats emerged immediately, flooding the tree's surface as they tried to escape from the light. My immediate reaction was to recoil, and in the seconds it took me to recover, most of them had already disappeared. In my resulting panic, I stabbed wildly at the tree, collecting several of the creatures on my blade before flicking them to the ground and doing so again. I kept going, not keeping count or looking at the pile, just stabbing and flicking until I found a rhythm.

The entire process couldn't have lasted more than thirty or forty seconds, but I was breathing like I'd just run a marathon. Lanir crouched and started gathering the armor rats in a pile, grunting his approval with his lip lifted into a smirk. "Should be plenty for a meal."

"Thank God for that." I slipped the blade back into its sheath, dropping to my knees beside Lanir and sucking in a deep breath. "Did I do okay?"

He chuckled. "You did amazing."

"I feel bad," I muttered, lifting one of the creatures' bodies and holding it in my palms. "I know I shouldn't, but I do."

When Lanir didn't respond, I looked up to find him staring at me, understanding in his eyes. "It's survival, S'mara… you ate meat on your planet?"

"Yes, I did, I just… I know, it's silly. I guess I've been separated from it because I've never had to kill for my meals before."

"You're sensitive, S'mara, and soft."

My brows furrowed, and I opened my mouth to protest, letting the words drop away unsaid at the look on his face. Lanir wasn't insulting me. He understood how I felt, maybe because he was a sensitive soul too. Deep down, I felt he was, and I wondered what the Ghaal had done to him to make the self-erected walls around himself so thick.

CHAPTER
20

LANIR

The aldaks cooked up well placed straight on the hot coals with their hard shells facing down. They cooked slowly and shrunk, but enough of them made a satisfying meal. I believe they are related to the eylaks, however distant, and were one of the few native creatures not wiped out by the Ghaal's chemical warfare.

S'mara smiled and talked as we ate, but now and then, she would descend into silence and look at her food or the pile of discarded shells, her lips pursed and eyes unfocused. I worried about her. She wasn't made for life on this planet, and from what she'd told me about her home, she had been well-protected. They lived in buildings in cities like the Ghaal used to have, although more condensed. Nature was restricted to certain areas—parklands and reserves—and humanity ruled the Earth on an increasingly fragile tip by the sounds of it. With finite resources and an ever-increasing population, I wondered if their planet would end up the same way as ours.

After we'd eaten, we cleaned our hands, and S'mara sat back down near the fire, glancing at the sky. "Is it going to rain?"

"Maybe." The air felt right, the slight shift in pressure, the taste of humidity dancing on every intake of breath.

"What will we do?"

I chuckled. She was *so fragile.* "Get wet."

S'mara reached out and shoved my arm playfully. "I know *that.*"

"We'll sleep nearer the trees, and I'll protect you as much as I can."

She nodded, poking at the glowing embers with a stick. "I'm sorry I'm not better at caring for myself."

A growl rumbled through my chest. "I like taking care of you."

I caught the whisper of a smile on her lips before it vanished, and my chest swelled with pride that I could make her smile, if only for a moment. "I don't want to be a burden. You've done so much for me. You've left your home—"

"My home is wherever I'm needed, and you need me."

She watched me for a drawn-out moment before offering me her beautiful smile. "You're so sweet."

Pushing herself to her knees, she shuffled over me, and when I didn't move, she pushed my arms out of the way so she could sit in my lap. Curling into a ball, she pressed her face against my chest and inhaled deeply, releasing a contented sigh as I wrapped my arms around her. When the growling started again, she chuckled and tapped my chest. "Why do you growl like that?"

"It's a reflex from one of the many types of DNA used to create us. A streak of possessiveness that makes us want to keep our mates close and safe. It also happens when our mates are happy or in danger. I can't stop it, but I can somewhat control it if you want it quieter?"

She giggled and pressed her ear against my chest. I shifted to allow her more room to move, her small fingers warm against my skin. When I focused on her body on top of mine, the feel of the curve of her ass and thighs against me, my cock hardened, and the growling increased.

S'mara released a small gasp. "What are you thinking about now?" she whispered, although I suspected she already knew.

"Fucking you," I growled out. This enticed another gasp from her, this one followed by a wiggle of her hips, creating friction against my cock that was both delicious and agonizing. My arms tightened around S'mara, torn between wanting to hold her still or grind back against her. "Careful, S'mara…"

"Why?" Her voice was muffled when her perfect lips pressed kisses against my chest. She then readjusted and straddled me so she could wrap her arms around my neck.

"Because I want to take you even when you're not teasing me."

She giggled again. "I've never teased anyone before." S'mara planted another few kisses against my neck, pausing before she dragged her lips across my skin, and her small tongue darted out and tasted me. She paused again as if deciding what to do before she gently bit into my shoulder enough to draw a groan from me. "It's kinda fun."

I chuckled, and the sound descended into another growl when she ran her tongue up my cheek, and she laughed at my reaction. I was happy to let her play. I doubted there was anything she could do that wouldn't feel good. Her body still felt so fragile and utterly breakable in my hands as my fingers wrapped around her back, and I held her close to me. But the trust she had in me only served to fuel my need for her. Her hands explored too, running around my shoulders, arms, and back before moving to my chest. She liked to follow the shapes of my muscles with her fingertips, her eyes wide and filled with lust as she did.

S'mara traced the lines where my skin was red instead of deep gray and followed the cracked effect I'd developed through adaption to camouflage in the mountains until her fingers moved up my neck. I tilted my chin back to let her explore and resisted the urge to take her now but was unable to stop my fingertips from gripping where I held her hips. I met her eyes as she tilted my head back so she could run her fingers along my lips, her tongue darting out to lick her own as she did.

I couldn't wait and grabbed the back of her head to bring her lips to mine, opening my mouth to devour her moans as my tongue found hers, dancing and playing as she liked.

S'mara broke the kiss, gasping as her gaze found mine, full of heat and lust. "You interrupted my fun." She pouted.

With a snarl, I flipped over, taking her with me, and laid her under me, growling as she automatically wrapped her legs around my hips. "There are other ways to have fun."

S'mara sighed, her swollen lips curved into a satisfied smile as she delicately traced the lines on my arms, holding my eye contact. "Show me."

Growling, I ripped off my loincloth—even the small piece of material was too much of a barrier between S'mara and me. Hiking up her tunic, I moved down to tongue at her nipples, groaning as they hardened under my touch. I couldn't wait, not tonight. Moving over her again, I gripped my cock, rubbing it up and down between her cunt's lips. She was already wet, and she squealed as I brushed her clit with the head of my cock. I repeated the motion until she was rocking her hips, desperate to come.

She was comfortable and knew I wouldn't hurt her.

S'mara trusted me.

To her, I wasn't an animal or a monster, and despite her being abducted from another planet, she had put all her trust and faith in me to care for her. I would kill for her, die for her, and burn everything down to get her back if she were taken from me.

I couldn't stop watching her as I thrust my hips against her, and she squirmed beneath me, gripping my shoulders as her breathing became heavy, laced with delicious moans and squeaks of pleasure every time I hit her clit. I loved that little nub—it was my favorite part of her body. Because even though her sweet cunt felt better around my cock than my hands ever would, that part of her made her explode with pleasure, and I wanted that for her more than anything.

One day, she'd be rounded with young, *our* young, and I would still pleasure her.

I groaned as S'mara came. She gasped, twitched, and reached down to push me away when the sensations became too much. But I pushed her through it and waited until she sighed after her orgasm, as she always did, before I readjusted and moved to slide my cock into her waiting cunt.

S'mara's grip on my shoulders increased, and her eyes flew open as the head of my cock penetrated her. She was so delectably tight. Her lips pursed and brows furrowed as I pushed in deeper. She screamed when I bottomed out with a hard thrust, and I dropped to my forearms, licking at her neck and cheek with the tip of my tongue.

"Did I hurt you?" I whispered, dread creeping up into my chest from my stomach. I stopped moving as S'mara squirmed around me, her legs falling open to accommodate my girth. "Do you want me to stop?"

"No," she whispered breathlessly, her eyes fluttering closed. I groaned as she shifted, bouncing slightly up and down on my cock, rocking her body underneath mine. I shuddered and traced a hand down her body so I could hold onto her hip. She needed to stop to allow her body time to adjust.

When I ceased my movements, S'mara whimpered. "Nooo, don't stop, *please.*"

Her cunt clenched around me. I snarled again

and grit my teeth. "Are you sure?"

"Lanir, please." She held my eye contact, bit, and let her teeth drag across her bottom lip. "Please… *fuck me.*"

The snarl that rose from my throat was beyond my control, and I gripped her hip, pulling out so I could snap my hips forward. Her body jerked beneath me, and she clenched around me again. I waited for a protest that didn't come and did it once more, fucking her harder than I had the first time. Her brows were still creased together, eyes closed, and lips permanently parted, but I kept moving, the slick wetness of her allowing me to thrust harder, the way I'd been dreaming when I imagined her cunt stretched around me.

The furrow of her brows eased, and S'mara arched her neck back, gasping and moaning as there was another flush of hot wetness from her surrounding my cock. Groaning, I moved harder and shuddered under the tight grip of her cunt. She was so small, yet she was taking everything I had to give. The longer I fucked her, the harder it was to slow down or stop, and S'mara's gasps and sounds of pleasure only drove me on.

Kneeling, I leaned back to watch my cock penetrate her as it stretched S'mara's sweet cunt to her limit. She moaned at the change of angle. The sight of her accepting me inside her almost had me coming undone, and I shifted to touch the little nub to bring her to her peak so we could come together. Growling, my thrusts became harder, and I closed my eyes, trying to keep control of myself so as not to hurt her. But S'mara reached forward and gripped my thighs, and when I opened my eyes, she was staring up at me. With the slightest nod, she spurred me on to use her as I needed.

I pressed harder against her clit, rubbing small, rough circles as I continued to pound into her while my other hand gripped her hip and held her to me as she shifted away with each thrust. Her cries grew louder, and when her cunt clamped down on me as she came, I lost control. Leaning over her, I planted my fists on either side of her head, tilting my hips and thrusting in harder and faster, the sounds of our skin slapping together all I could hear.

My vision blurred, and I snarled, snapping my jaws as I came, filling S'mara with my seed, pumping my cum in deeper, wanting to claim her ultimately as mine, to fill her with young.

She was perfect and was more than I deserved.

I knew the right thing to do was to bring her to her friends, but with her cunt stretched around me, all I wanted to do was keep her with me.

Because if she had the protection of her friends, would she still need me?

Would she still want me?

CHAPTER 21

SAMARA

The ache between my legs was ecstasy, and my cheeks flushed whenever I concentrated on it too much. Lanir would glance at me, his lip twitching as if he knew exactly what I was thinking.

Two nights ago, we'd had sex again, and I'd encouraged him to let go and fuck me how he wanted to. He'd moved hard and fast, and at first, my body struggled to accommodate him, but the pleasure overtook the discomfort, and every stretch as he penetrated me only made it feel better.

Last night, we'd done it again, and I'd straddled him and sunk onto his cock as he lay back, his hands gripping bruises into my thighs as I bounced on him. I still couldn't shake the image from my mind comparing Lanir to a demon. But when I looked down at him, lying under me, his bright green eyes blazed with lust as he watched me fuck him, I felt powerful.

And safe.

Lanir may have looked like a demon, but he was mine and would protect me as much as I would protect him.

I'd try to anyway, although physically, there was nothing I could offer in the way of protection he couldn't do himself.

We kept moving yesterday, working our way farther along the border of the woodlands that thickened as we got closer to the forest in the distance. We'd stopped at a stream to refill our water bags and bathe. The pace was leisurely but not without tension. Every now and then Lanir would snatch my arm and change direction, steering me away from where I thought we were headed. Sometimes we'd retrace our steps, moving in a large circle. But he never pushed me harder than I could handle, and I was grateful.

Lanir stopped to collect some lunch for us, and I wandered around the edge of the woods, making sure to always keep him in my sight. I'd learned my lesson more than once about the dangers of this planet.

So when I found myself face to face with another female, I should have been more afraid.

She stepped out from the tree line into my path, forcing me to stop short. We ended up nearly chest to chest, and the similarities in our builds forced a shudder down my spine. I didn't need Lanir to tell me this was another abducted species. She was humanoid too—two arms, two legs. Her skin was the yellow of a wheat field and covered in a thin layer of almost translucent fur. She was naked, and the swell of four breasts under her fur was clear. Shapely hips and thighs rounded out her figure, and when I made no move to flee, she bared her teeth at me. Her mouth was bright red as if filled with blood, and I recoiled slightly.

I felt Lanir move in behind me, and the female alien looked up at him and repeated the motion of baring her teeth, a strange gurgling sound coming forth.

In a move that surprised me, Lanir leaned forward, opened his arms wide, and snarled at her, loud and aggressive, the sound similar to how he'd reacted when we were faced with the Ghaal. I stood in shock for a moment as the female fled, and only turned when Lanir moved away from behind me.

"Why did you do that?" Lanir looked up from where he'd been collecting root berries and stopped to add them to the pile of fruits he'd already collected while I'd been wandering. He didn't answer, and I approached him, asking again, "Why did you scare her like that? I don't think she meant any harm."

"I'm sure she didn't."

"Lanir, please. We've talked about you drip-feeding me information. Just tell me."

Lanir sank to his knees and grabbed my tunic, forcing me to sit next to him before shoving a piece of fruit in my hands. "I don't know the name of her species... I was unable to communicate with them." I began eating when he stared hard at me, and I waited for him to continue. "They were skittish, and I couldn't get near them to connect with their minds. They'd landed closer to Eldich's home and made their way to near my cave. I had to scare them away from the Ghaal colony, and without the ability to communicate, all I could do was frighten them." Lanir turned his green eyes on me, devoid of emotion, like he'd shut himself down again. "I need her to still fear me, so that's why I acted as I did. I don't want them anywhere near my cave... it's too close to the colony. They're safer here in the woods."

"But the Ghaal are after me and my friends now. They won't be interested in her."

Lanir looked to where she'd disappeared into the trees. "Perhaps, but I can't take the chance they won't still want to use her for experiments." His expression darkened, and I paused midbite at the intensity of his gaze. "Or spare parts."

Dropping the piece of fruit, my hunger had evaporated with his words. "Lanir?" He grunted, huffing out a breath through his nose, but didn't speak. "When are we going to try to find my friends?"

He shifted his intense gaze from where the furry, yellow female had disappeared to me and lost none of the storm behind his eyes. I shifted under his scrutiny, unable to tell what he was thinking. His hands and arms twitched as though he was resisting the urge to grab me. I frowned, about to ask again when he spoke.

"We'll start circling today and head back toward the mountains toward Ilk's."

"Okay." I didn't know what else to say. Something had changed. More things he wasn't telling me.

Not wanting to waste the food he'd foraged, I finished eating, wiped my fingers on my tunic, and took a drink of fresh water.

Lanir would tell me what he was hiding when he was ready.

I was sure of it.

True to his word, we turned west. Or what I assumed was West. We changed direction away from the woodlands and began crossing the fields, passing through rocky outcrops that peeked up between the long grasses.

Lanir was walking stiffly, no longer moving with the grace he had through the mountains and even around the outskirts of the woodlands. His gaze was unfocused, and he moved as though his mind was elsewhere. Perhaps on the memories he refused to share with me. I wanted him to tell me. Whatever happened, whatever it was that plagued him, if he told me, then he wouldn't be carrying the burden himself. Bit by bit, he had opened up, revealing a being much more complex than I could have predicted when I first laid eyes on him.

I wanted to help him as he had helped me.

When we reached a clearing, I stopped, taking a moment to examine the rock formations surrounding the area. This wasn't natural—the stone was too smooth, the pathways too focused— and although bushes, vines, and grasses were growing from every nook and crevice, this was definitely not a natural structure.

Lanir was already moving past the pathways,

and I reached forward and grabbed his hand.

"Can we take a look?" I asked. I suspected this was a remnant of the Ghaal civilization that used to cover this planet before they wiped each other out. I'd noticed remnants of other buildings along our journey—crumbling stone walls and jagged pieces of metal I didn't recognize sticking up from the ground—but this was the first time I'd seen something that looked like it was designed to be hidden. Not a field of houses or workplaces or whatever the other ruins were, but a pathway hidden amongst stone.

Lanir's jaw was taut even as he nodded.

I watched him for a moment longer. "If you don't want to, we don't have to."

His eyes narrowed as he glanced down the pathway, his eyes seeming to clear as he took in the scenery around him. The furrow in his brow returned, accompanied by a darkening expression that made him look dangerous—a look I would have recalled if I didn't know him well enough to feel utterly safe in his presence. "I didn't intend to bring you this way," he muttered.

Frowning, I shook my head. "Lanir, please, I don't understand. You're giving me only snippets of the story, bits and pieces of what you're thinking. I thought we were past this. We were closer than this. Can you please talk to me?"

He studied me the same way he did when he first

brought me back to his cave, and I sat against the opposite wall, trembling. An expression I couldn't read as his eyes blazed with intensity and his pupils had blown. He'd be pulling away from me for the past day, and even more so since we came across that other abducted female. Reaching out, I grabbed his hand, and Lanir was startled at the contact.

"Memories brought me here," he said simply, staring down the pathway again between the rocks. "I had no intention of walking this way, but it seems the memories of this place were so ingrained in me, I had no choice."

"Like muscle memory?" Lanir glanced at me, and I studied his eyes, waiting for the darkness behind his expression to dissipate. It didn't. "You've been here before, and without even knowing, your body brought you back here." I squeezed his hand. "Maybe part of you needed to be here... needed to see it." I glanced down the pathway, wondering what lay there and mumbling, "Whatever this place is."

A growl rumbled through his chest as his lip lifted into a snarl. "This is where I was created."

A small *oh* escaped my lips, and I was torn between wanting to see what lay beyond and not wanting Lanir to be reminded of whatever happened to him here. But without another word, he moved down the pathway, gripped my hand, and pulled me along behind him. The pathway narrowed, and the tall purple and gray dappled rocks towered over me on both sides, making me shudder as claustrophobia took hold. I released a breath with a sigh when the pathway opened again, and I was presented with a building that looked to be partially collapsed. But as I stared, I realized maybe it was intended to look like that—the strange dark metal sticking out of the ground at odd angles, coming together to form a haphazard peak, like a tent with too many sides.

Lanir was trembling, and I was about to ask if he wanted to turn back, but before I could speak, he started determinedly moving forward, his angry steps loud here where the rocks cut out all the sounds of nature from around us.

He shrugged off all the supplies he'd be carrying near the building's entrance, and cautiously, I followed suit. "There won't be any Ghaal here, will there?"

His responding snarl was animalistic, and I flinched. "I wouldn't have brought you here if they were." He rounded on me, and his expression softened when he saw my widened eyes, but only a hint. "This is a shell of a building. They cleared out all technology long ago. All Ghaal live in the colony between the mountains and the ocean."

"So, there's nothing inside at all?" I whispered, and even the whisper echoed around the strange foyer veranda that curved overhead.

"Only memories." Lanir sneered, visibly trembling now with fear or anger, I couldn't tell. "And nightmares."

Lanir's cryptic answers had me on the verge of telling him I had changed my mind and didn't want to go inside the abandoned building anymore. A place full of nightmares for him? No, thank you. But Lanir took my hand and pulled me through the large entrance, where doors may have once been but were no longer, now only a crumbling opening. I tried to recall how long it had been since the Ghaal was reduced to a single colony—generations Lanir had said—decades upon decades since the war, unable to maintain the cities that once covered this land. Nature had taken over, and now only ghosts of the buildings remained.

Like this one—haunted with memories.

Frowning, I tried to focus as the light faded the farther we went into the building. There was no artificial light, only the gaps in the crumbling ceiling allowing sunlight to stream through.

"Lanir?" I whispered, unsure why I was whispering. There was no one else around, but this felt like a wicked place where to speak too loudly would be to summon the ghosts who lived in the shadows. Lanir hummed in response but said nothing. "Why were you created here and not at the colony if that's where all the Ghaal lived?"

Without looking at me, he answered like a

machine delivering information with no emotion or inflection in his deep, rumbling tone. "We were an experiment. The remaining population was too precious to risk if something went wrong. Out here, if there were an accident, only a few would perish."

I nodded, hating that all I wanted to do was ask more questions, but Lanir seemed to be drifting further inside himself the farther we ventured into the building. Who was I to bring up more traumatic memories? Lanir owed me nothing and had already saved my life more than once. To question him further about his origins and how he escaped seemed wrong and intrusive.

He'd told me he would tell me when he was ready, one day, and that wasn't up to me to decide.

The walls were smooth and dark, and the damage from age appeared more to be peeling away at the walls rather than the crumbling I would expect from stone or concrete on Earth. In some places, the walls were so thin that the light came through, sending an eerie blue glow across the floor. There were tables covered in vines and soil and other plants. Small animals moved around the floor, skittering out of sight if we came too close.

Lanir came to an abrupt halt, and I ran into his back, releasing a squeak when he squeezed my hand. I managed to pull my fingers from his grip, stepping out behind Lanir as he pressed his hands against the side of a clear tube.

A tube big enough for him to fit in.

"Lanir?" I breathed out his name, not sure if I should break the spell he was under.

Lanir ran a hand across the tube, clearing the vines and dust out of the way, and stared at his reflection.

Then his eyes rolled up into his head, and I screamed as he collapsed.

CHAPTER 22

LANIR

My brothers watched me cautiously.

We decided we were brothers and family, although there was no proof of DNA linking us— it was more than that. We wanted to be a family and more than bodies designed to breed. Enhanced empathy and intelligence were only side effects of the Ghaal trying to create a stronger version of themselves.

We were different from the Ghaal, enough we could sleep soundly at night with clear consciences.

When they let us sleep.

But we didn't want to breed.

The Ghaal DNA was strong, and if two Synths bred, the offspring would be Ghaal, the DNA programmed to attract, to override the synthetic DNA created to make us stronger. The Ghaal we birthed would be a stronger version of their race, but most certainly Ghaal. They'd discussed breeding us with other species or at least attempting to, but that would result in a Synth hybrid, and they didn't want that.

They wanted more Ghaal, and the only reason we were created.

My brothers watched me because I was the first to show signs of changing gender, of becoming female. A change we had tried to fight, but much like our ability to adapt to our environments, a change we ultimately couldn't help. Kept in each other's presence long enough, it was only a matter of time before one or more of us changed.

The scent of female hormones was all around me. Physically, I looked the same as my brothers— a blank slate of a Ghaal, same skin, but without the orange eyes—a template. But I was different now, my body was forcing me to become female, to open up the possibility for breeding. We were created that way. It was inevitable.

We often spoke of escaping, but then what? We would have to live apart. Being together would only mean the changes continued, the breeding would happen, and we would birth offspring.

Ghaal offspring. The very consequence we were trying to avoid.

I cowered in the corner while Ilk and Eldich stood protectively in front of me as I writhed, unable to sleep as the changes increased in speed—my waist slimmer, hips wider, and hormones changing. The hormones were the most dangerous change of all. They called to my brothers—the other males caged with me—and enticed them.

And their hormones, I couldn't bear it. A scent I had barely taken notice of only days ago was now so strong I wept as I turned my head away and buried my face between the wall and my hands, trying to block out the smell that called to me— the scent that enticed my body, my hormones responding to theirs.

I couldn't stop the changes. No amount of willpower or stubbornly insisting to myself I would remain male could stop them. The Ghaal watched in glee as they sensed the changes, testing our blood daily and mine every few hours once they realized I was the one who would change to female first.

The weak link.

I would be as strong as a female Synth as I was male, but the weakness was in my willpower and my inability to control the change, or at least hold it off long enough for us to escape.

Vitri was the first to break.

The scent of my female hormones became too much for him, and he launched himself across the cage at me, slamming into Ilk and Ryth while Sahcor and Eldich tried to hold him back. But he was animal, and Eldich's eyes were also rolling as he too fought the urges. His grip on Vitri was lax, not really holding him back but wishing he could.

His mind fighting his body, he was as ashamed of his weakness as I was mine.

"Move!" Vitri snarled as I backed against the wall, allowing Ilk and Ryth to shield me while at the same time hating myself for it.

I should be fighting my own fight.

But I didn't trust myself to.

Vitri and I locked eyes, his gaze dark and wild, and I tilted up my chin, my body inviting him to me.

I wanted him.

I wanted to mate.

I needed it.

Vitri picked up on my body language, and a surge of male pheromones flooded the air, making me gasp and bite back a moan. Pinning myself against the cage's wall, I clawed at it, desperate to escape the urges I couldn't control. We may be intelligent, but our instincts would eventually take over.

We would all be lost to our animalistic desires to mate and breed, one after the other, until the Ghaal got what they wanted—male and female offspring to interbreed with the remaining population. Offspring not affected by the infertility issues remaining from the war. Offspring to increase the gene pool and bring the species back from the edge of extinction.

So they could destroy themselves all over again.

No.

"Vitri, no." I held out my hand between us as though it would make a difference if he came for me because I wouldn't fight him. The second his skin touched mine, I would be lost, the change would complete, and we would mate. Recognition flashed across Vitri's eyes, and he stopped fighting against Ilk for a moment. But then the pheromones came back stronger, drawing us together, and I pressed myself against Ilk, desperate to be closer to Vitri.

Ilk roared and, with a palm against my shoulder, slammed me against the wall.

We fought like that for hours, Vitri and I getting closer before being pulled apart, indecision plastered across Eldich's face as he witnessed the chaos. His hands were gripped into fists, shaking with the effort not to come too close.

He would be the next to change.

The Ghaal came to check on us throughout the day, and every time, they grew more impatient that we weren't mating yet. They would scream at Ilk, brandishing their only weapon against us in our faces—a small handheld instrument that, if pressed into our skin, would release a toxin that would essentially shut us down. The toxin would flood our body, attaching to every bit of Synth DNA and destroying it, and within minutes, we would be dead. The weapon did nothing to the Ghaal DNA and couldn't be used against them. It was our weakness and their only means of control over us.

"We created you, and we can destroy you." They would remind us when we refused to cooperate with their experiments.

But even that threat fell on deaf ears this time while we continued to fight against each other. Vitri and I tried and almost failed to fight against our own urges to come together and mate.

Eventually, the cage door was opened, and I was dragged from it, the toxin wand held at my back.

My breathing slowed the farther I was from Vitri, and I could hear his anguished roaring echoing down the hall even when I could no longer see him. The Ghaal prodded me with their fingers, shoving me into a separate room and another cage.

This one for torture.

I was familiar with this room but too wound up trying to deny my urges that I didn't react until I was already in the tube. My first instinct was to lash out until they'd brandish that wand, and I'd back into the tube, allowing them to close the curved door over me even as I snarled and snapped at them.

"You can't continue to fight the urge to mate," one of them said. *I never bothered to learn their names—why would I? My brothers and I had named ourselves rather than the digits they assigned us.* *"Look at your body... you're practically female. You should just give in."*

A roar ripped from me as I clung to the one tiny part of male hormones I could sense, holding on tight and refusing to let go, almost biting through my tongue in the process.

I would not *become female.*

I would not *put my brothers through that agony of being so close to me and trying to resist.*

I would not *be the reason we failed in our conviction.*

I couldn't help that I was the first to start the change, the weakest-willed, but I would fight with every fiber of my being.

I would not *willingly give the Ghaal what they wanted.*

When I didn't respond, the Ghaal released an angry click through its teeth. "Use your words... you're not an animal."

With a snarl, I found the strength to answer. "I am what you made me."

The Ghaal stared at me for a beat longer, orange eyes on my green.

"You will submit," one said and hovered his hand over the silver ball next to the tube containing me, activating the device.

White-hot pain shot through my body, burning at every nerve ending. I screamed, my body transforming on the spot, desperate to make the pain stop but unable to turn off the machine. My skin changed, hardened, then changed texture. My body fought, and the rapid change was harrowing. I tried not to scream and to hold the agony inside me. I didn't want the Ghaal to know the pain was getting to me and for them to think this treatment would help them win against our will.

The way they created us was doing that already, and every day we were together was becoming harder to endure. I loved my brothers. We were bonded through circumstance and creation. We were created at the same time, in the same moment, brought to consciousness and made aware of the world. We were told of our purpose—adapting and learning together, realizing the things we could do when the Ghaal forced information into us—their history and knowledge of science and technology, everything they thought would help us be sympathetic to their cause. They thought if we knew, we would want to help, but all we saw was a violent species who, even before the wars, never treated each other or any creatures with respect. Violence, rape, and murder were rampant among the population and were never punished, only seen as the strong surviving and the weak being culled.

The pain increased with a resonating hum added to it, vibrating through me, and finally, I released the scream I had been trying to hold inside. I couldn't hear anything over my own voice, not even sure what was my voice or the machine anymore.

Hours.

Days.

They released me from the machine long enough to blast me with icy water, which I drank and gulped at gratefully as if dying. I suppose maybe I was. They'd ask if I was ready to comply, and I would attack.

Then I'd be back in the machine.

I took all the punishment because as long as the Ghaal was focused on me, they wouldn't realize Vitri was the first to lose control and try to mate with me and that Eldich wasn't far behind me, and the slightest tang of female hormones was detectable on his scent.

They treated me like an animal, and that's all I became.

How long it was before we eventually managed to escape, I couldn't be sure. Time had little meaning when most days I was dragged between a torture chamber and back into the cage with my brothers, barely conscious. Perhaps the Ghaal hoped Vitri would mate me while I couldn't fight back. But even when Vitri lost control, Sahcor was edging on control himself, and Eldich's own female hormones became more apparent, we didn't give in.

Our escape was only loosely planned, but one day when they opened the cage to take me away, something inside me broke. There would be no more torture of my brothers or me, no more forcing us in together, knowing our instincts would eventually take over. They cursed the grave of the scientist who created us for making us intelligent enough to have willpower and desires of our own.

No more.

The second the Ghaal's hands were on me, mine

were on his head, and I twisted until I heard the satisfying crack of his neck breaking. The Ghaal crumbled, the toxin wand flew from his hand and clattered across the floor. I launched at the next, sinking my teeth into his neck and gripping, then yanked my head back, ripped his flesh away, and spat his sickly blood from my mouth. There was shouting, but I couldn't hear what was being said. I didn't care. I turned around long enough to see my brothers had followed me out of the cage and made my way through the Ghaal coming out of the other labs. I killed without hesitation, without mercy, and before we made it to the front door, the Ghaal had simply backed away and were letting us go. Their numbers were too few, too precious to take too many deaths at our hands. My skin was streaked with their blood as I burst outside into the sun, blinking against the onslaught of light. I heard Ilk call my name and turned to face him, roaring when he came too close.

I needed to be alone to get control over my body and turn back into me.

I would find my brothers later.

I hoped I communicated all of this to Ilk through the look, unable to find the words, my mind a haze and nothing but animal desires and cravings.

Food. Sex. Water. Food. Sex.

So, I ran.

Ilk found me more than a month later.

I'd returned to male and lived alone and off the land, moving around constantly, never making a home. I'd picked up the scent of my brothers near the mountains and stayed away.

The Ghaal hadn't come after me, and if they'd made a move to recover my brothers, I wasn't aware of it. Perhaps we were a lost cause, the last experiment of a dying Ghaal, and a pipedream that would never have worked anyway. But I needed to be sure I wouldn't change again before joining my brothers and be certain there were no female hormones left in me. Gripping the tree in front of me, I watched Ilk, ready to tell him I wouldn't be the reason Vitri was tempted and tortured. Eying Ilk wearily as he approached, I was crouched and ready to attack. I hated that my instinct was to attack, but I knew nothing else now. Everyone who came for me was to inflict pain, and my only response was violence. I didn't want to lash out and hurt Ilk on an instinct that had been so ingrained in me that it was almost as strong as the instinct to mate.

"Lanir..." Ilk's voice was calm and smooth, with a deep rumbling through him. He sniffed the air,

and satisfied there wasn't the scent of female hormones, took another step toward me with his hand outstretched. "Come. We've made a home for ourselves in the mountains."

"We can't be together," I growled out.

Ilk's expression was pained. He knew I spoke the truth. "We've been separating every few days, coming back together when we can." But there was tension in his muscles, and he knew the arrangement couldn't last. We were a family doomed never to be able to be together. We couldn't stop our bodies from changing— willpower only went so far—and we wouldn't be responsible for bringing more Ghaal to life. "I think we'll be needed soon."

Standing, the tree branches shifted out of the way as my shoulders shoved past them. "What do you mean?"

Ilk's jaw tensed. "The Ghaal won't give up trying to find a way, and we've seen transport ships hanging around the atmosphere, close enough to make contact..." He drifted off as I snarled at his implication—the Ghaal was going to search for compatible females elsewhere.

With a twitch of my lip, I stepped toward Ilk, and he moved as though he were going to embrace me before changing his mind. "Vitri?" I asked simply, blurting out the word.

"Under control."

A jerk of my chin and a huff of air through my nose was all the acknowledgment I offered him, and I indicated for him to move so I could follow him back to the home they'd made, however temporary. I was not sure I would ever truly relax around my brothers again, knowing the weakness I held within me and the danger I posed to them, destined to bring out their instincts purely from my proximity.

I'd stay with them, but not for long.

I was better off alone.

CHAPTER 23

SAMARA

Lanir didn't respond when I screamed his name, and I foolishly ran toward him as he collapsed.

His weight fell on me, and there was no way I was strong enough to stop him from collapsing, so I went down with him and managed to maneuver enough so only his head was on my outstretched legs and I wasn't trapped beneath his bulk. His limbs jerked and twitched, and his eyelids flickered as though he were having a violent dream or a seizure.

I brushed my fingers over his cheek and

forehead and whispered his name repeatedly. "Lanir, please wake up. I'm sorry I asked you to come here. That was *so* stupid." Tears filled my eyes and spilled onto my cheeks as my vision blurred. "Whatever they did to you, you've suffered so much. I'm so sorry." I glanced around the room, taking in the large tube big enough to hold Lanir and the table, which maybe once held instruments of torture. "Oh, Lanir, what did they do to you?"

The weight of him was making my toes tingle, but I didn't dare move and focused instead on his steady breathing as his body's jerking motions slowed. I continued to talk to him, hoping something was getting through. After what felt like an eternity but was perhaps only half an hour, I maneuvered enough to get the extra water bag, drinking some myself before trickling some onto Lanir's lips.

But he didn't wake.

My attention was pulled from Lanir when a scuttling sound got too close for comfort, and my eyes darted around the semi-lit room as I tracked the movement of the leaves and small plants.

Something was circling us, and I gnawed at my lip.

Sliding out from under Lanir, I gently placed his head on the floor and rolled him onto his side so he didn't swallow his tongue like I'd learned in my first-aid class years ago. Glancing around, I grabbed the only weapon I could see aside from my knife, which felt laughably small now that I was alone, and snatched up Lanir's spear. It was heavy and felt misbalanced, and the head of it tilted off-center as I struggled to keep it upright. Placing myself in front of Lanir, an ugly snorting now accompanied the shuffling sound, and I held the spear in front of me, ready to stab at anything that approached.

Something sprung at me, bouncing off two large hind legs and launching like a live cannonball. I screamed, thrust the spear forward, and caught it through its stomach. The creature screeched and writhed, and I shook the spear, trying to dislodge it as more grunting and scuffling surrounded us. The creature looked almost like a beaver, except for the layers of razor-sharp teeth that circled its mouth threateningly as it squealed before it died. My hand trembled as I reached out to remove it from the end of the spear, kicking it away and fighting back tears.

No. This was no time to cry.

Another one came at me from behind, and I swung fast enough to hit it with the side of the spearhead and sent it flying, hitting the ground with a hard crunch and sliding before it jumped back onto its legs. The sounds it made were driving me crazy—screaming, screeching, and snorting as it exposed its teeth at me, chomping them menacingly. It was the size of a medium dog, all bulk and muscle.

If I had to fight it off by hand, I felt I could.

Maybe.

But several of them? Definitely not.

"Oh my God, oh my God, *oh my God*," I muttered and spun around as several more emerged from the plant life that wound around the tables and the remainder of the deteriorating building.

One sob escaped my throat—only one—before I grunted out a sound of determination.

No. I wouldn't give up.

Lanir had protected me.

I was on an *alien planet.*

If ever there was a time to bring myself together, now was it.

Leaning toward a group of three as they hopped closer, I drew in a deep breath. "Go *away!*" I screamed, holding the note as long as possible and adding as much volume and screech as I could manage. The creatures stopped moving, eyeing me wearily, and their teeth clicked against each other as they moved their jaws around. I swung the spear toward another group, screaming again. No words this time, just an animalistic scream. Stabbing at one of them, I nicked it with the end of the spear, and it screeched angrily at me. I screamed back, raising my arms above my head and stomping my feet.

One to my right made another attempt to attack and launched itself from its feet. I stabbed out and downward, losing control of the spear when the weight of the creature was added to it. It was driven into the floor, killing the creature instantly with a harsh stab. The others clicked angrily, and I screamed again, wrenching the spear from the dead one and brandishing it at them.

"I'll kill every one of you if I have to!" I cried.

Two attacked at once, and I managed to knock one away as the other landed on Lanir, immediately moving to sink its rows of teeth into Lanir's leg. "Oh… no you don't." Stabbing out again, it hopped out of the way, but not before I managed to pierce through the muscle of its thick leg. The others began backing up, and I continued to scream and stab out at them until they disappeared back into the plants. I only relaxed when the shuffling of the leaves had moved away from us and collapsed to my knees, my hand still gripped around the spear, my knuckles white.

My breathing came in heavy gasps as the adrenaline ebbed away, and impatiently, I wiped away the tears on my cheeks.

I did it. I almost laughed in relief. *I'd protected Lanir.*

Fear crawled up my gut at the idea there might be larger predators around that were only kept at bay by Lanir's presence, or the beaver aliens might come back. I whipped around to face Lanir and crawled toward him, brushed his forehead again, and recoiled my hand when I realized my skin was splattered with greenish-gray blood.

"Lanir?" I whispered, trying to shake the blood from my hand as I trembled. "Please wake up."

His eyelids fluttered, and he stirred and snarled when I touched his forehead. Lanir's arm lashed out and gripped my wrist, making me scream with surprise. When his eyes opened, and he focused on my face, his grip on my wrist eased. But he didn't let go. Instead, he pulled me forward until I lost balance, his other hand coming up to grab my hair as he guided my lips to his. The kiss was hungry and greedy, and he was growling as he took my month, plunging in his tongue until I gasped for air. Just as quickly as he'd initiated the kiss, Lanir pulled away and jerked into a crouching position before he shuffled away from me.

Still on my hands and knees, I crawled closer to him, reaching out my fingers when he flinched away from me.

"Thank God you're okay," I whispered, trying to keep my voice steady as I pulled back and swiped away more tears. "What happened?"

His pupils were dilated and darted around the room, taking me in—the blood from the creatures, the bodies of the ones I'd killed, the tube behind him, and back to me again.

"I don't deserve you, S'mara," he grumbled, his voice rough and edged with pain.

I dropped my hand, sat back on my heels, and watched him. "I was so worried," I said, pressing my lips together when he shook his head.

"Can you forgive me for being so weak?"

"Weak?" I didn't understand. "You're the strongest man I know."

He shook his head again, then his whole body, like a dog trying to shake away water, but I got the impression he was trying to disperse horrible thoughts, to rid himself of the memories and nightmares that haunted this place and him. As he stood, I didn't give him a chance to speak further and launched myself at him before I wrapped my arms around his waist. He stilled, his breathing increased, and his heart thumped loudly against my ear.

"I don't care about your weird, cryptic answers right now," I muttered against his chest and breathed in his wonderful scent. "I'm just so glad you're okay."

A world of things played across his face when I tilted my head up to look at him before he slowly wrapped his arms around me and pulled me against him.

CHAPTER 24

LANIR

S'mara clung to me. Her small hands grabbed at my back as though she were trying to pull me closer when we were as close as we could be. She was covered in blood, and the bodies of several barda were strewn around. They must have attacked, and she fended them off and killed several.

While *I* was unconscious.

Once again, I had failed her and not looked after her as I should.

The thought sent waves of anger and self-loathing through me, initiating the growling in my chest. S'mara hummed contently at the growl, rubbed her face against my skin, and breathed in my scent. My cock grew hard at the closeness of her warm body, and I tried to ignore it.

Being back here had proven too much.

The memories were one thing, but they were something I could bury away most of the time. What I was unable to shake was how the things that happened had shaped me—the anger and resulting violence. I never meant to come this way, although it was the quickest way to circle back to the mountains to find Ilk. I had avoided most of the relics of the Ghaal buildings as S'mara and I traveled, but something had drawn me here, a memory buried so deep it lived in my muscles. Muscle memory, exactly as S'mara had said.

The tube they had used to torture me brought everything back, and I was so overwhelmed with the memories of fear, anger, and hopelessness. I was overwhelmed with the guilt of being the weakest, that I was weak once again, and my mind shut down to try to deal with it all.

Meanwhile, S'mara was here, fighting off creatures that were no threat to me but could have injured or killed her.

She fought for me.

For. Me.

She was much more than I deserved, and I didn't know how to tell her. S'mara kept telling me I was giving her cryptic responses. But I'd gone so long without conversation and having to explain my thoughts or actions to anyone that sometimes finding the words was difficult.

Yet she was still here, patiently waiting for me to be ready.

"More than I deserve..." I muttered.

S'mara looked up, angling her chin onto my chest to stare at me. "Are you ready to tell me what happened?"

There was no accusation in her voice, no pressure or anger, only softness and patience. My gentle S'mara, who could wield a spear when needed and kill and protect me, was simply waiting for me to be ready.

She'd waited more than enough. I unwrapped her arms from me and collected my spear and our supplies. "I will tell you everything, S'mara," I grumbled, taking her hand. "But let's leave this place first."

We'd found a quiet place away from the rocky outcrops surrounding the Ghaal's abandoned laboratory near a small stream that trickled through the fields and sparse trees. I helped her wash her arms and face free of the barda blood, then S'mara sat cross-legged next to me and leaned against me with her hands tracing lines along my skin as I spoke. I told her everything. Why the Ghaal created us, the torture, and my weakness at being the first to change. This was the hardest part to tell her, that my brothers had been able to fight off the changes longer than me, and I was the one who broke Vitri's will to fight his instincts. S'mara didn't flinch nor look at me differently, but simply continued to touch me with small, reassuring contact. I told her of our escape and the subsequent abduction of other species and how we tried to help.

I told her everything—right up until the moment I took her from the unit that landed.

I was weak again in not trying to destroy the Ghaal colony. I knew Ilk didn't want violence, and I knew the Ghaal had the technology to kill us in an instant, but we should have done more.

I would change Ilk's mind—it was time for a war of our own.

When I finished talking, S'mara continued to rub my arm gently before she snaked her fingers down and took my hand, interlacing her fingers in mine.

After a beat of silence, I asked, "Do you hate me?"

Her eyes shot up to mine. "Why on earth would I hate you?"

"Because I'm weak. I'm the weakest of my

brothers. I was the first to change. I started the chain reaction that caused us to fight daily."

"Lanir, you're looking at it all wrong." I furrowed my brow at her, unable to stand looking at her for too long, a reminder of beauty I didn't deserve, and instead stared out over the horizon toward the mountains in the distance. "You weren't weak. You were *strong.* So strong." When I snarled, a reaction I couldn't help, she patted my hand. "You took all that pain, everything the Ghaal gave you, and you didn't break. Not only that, you refused to put your brothers in danger, leaving to be alone when you thought your presence would harm them. And that couldn't have been easy, being alone all that time when all you really needed was support."

She shook her head as her lip trembled, her voice shaking. "So much pain, so much cruelty."

When I didn't look at her, she lifted a hand and grabbed my chin, and I relented, letting her guide me to look into her eyes.

"And you came out the other end and still felt with such intensity that you fell for the human woman you found before me instantly. You felt *love* after everything you'd been through. That's strength."

I watched her, taking in the way the sunlight brought out all the colors in her eyes. It didn't feel like strength but like another weakness to me. To feel so intensely, so much so fast, made me weak.

This is what made me the first to lose the fickle control we had over our bodies and instincts.

S'mara smiled at me, a smile that reflected her gentle nature. "You don't believe me."

When I huffed out a breath through my nose, she shook her head, and her soft smile never wavered.

"We'll cut straight through toward Ilk's today. We may even make it there by tomorrow or the following morning."

"Okay." Her voice was far away, and I watched her as she gazed into the distance toward the mountains where we would begin our journey to find her friends. "Even when we find the other girls, you'll stay with me... right?"

My muscles tensed where she rubbed my arm, and I stared straight ahead and clenched my jaw. "You want me to stay with you?"

S'mara ducked her head against my arm, snuggling against me while I sat still, already feeling my heart rate increase and my pheromones begin to strengthen. "Of course. I like you. I care about you."

When I glanced at her, her cheeks were flushed pink again as she looked down. I followed her gaze, my loincloth again tented with my arousal. I needed to take her again, but with the vivid reminder of the nightmares I have lived through brought back to the forefront of my mind, now all I saw was every element of me as a weakness. Every temptation given into, every desire to fuck S'mara was nothing more than me not being able to control myself when I should be able to.

"You like me too, I see," S'mara muttered with a small chuckle. When she glanced at my face, her smile fell away, and she reached up, smoothing out the furrow in my brow with her thumb. "Please don't hate yourself, Lanir. You don't deserve all the judgment you give yourself." She wrapped her small hand around my cock, and I jumped, thrusting my hips forward into her touch, groaning loudly. "I can't make the memories go away, but—"

"You can." I was growling and surprised she was able to pick up I had spoken at all.

"What do you mean?"

"You make the bad memories go away."

She started pumping my cock in her hand and pulled away only long enough to flick the cloth out of the way. The skin-on-skin contact seared and wiped all the doubts and hatred from my mind once again. Every touch of her was soft and soothing, and every scent and taste pushed away all the darkness inside. When we locked eyes, she was smiling at me again, and with a snarl, I lurched forward, twisting my torso around so I could capture her mouth in mine, fucking her mouth with my tongue the way she liked. S'mara moaned into the kiss. I lifted her onto my lap and tugged her tunic out of the way so I could rub my erect length against her cunt. She was already wet, and when she opened her legs to straddle me, her scent wafted over me, making me shudder. Pulling away, I watched S'mara's eyelids flutter as she breathed in deeply and took in the scent of my pheromones, letting them intoxicate her the way she intoxicated me.

Gripping her hips, I lifted as she reached down to grab my cock, guiding it into her. She screamed when I pulled her down against me and penetrated her deeply in one single thrust. My snarl turned into a roar, and S'mara clung to me, wrapped her arms around my neck, and buried her face against my skin as I moved her on me. She weighed nothing to me, and I'd never tire of the feel of her smooth skin under my hands. I couldn't help gripping her harder and shuddered at the way she opened up for me, every thrust bringing another flush of wetness from her slick cunt.

"My mate..." I murmured and licked a long, languid stroke up her neck, "... my mate... *mine...*" S'mara nodded against me, panting and moaning. "Come around my cock, S'mara."

She nodded again. I shifted my legs to change angles, driving up into her faster, and her thighs slapped against mine. S'mara brought her hand between us, keeping her other arm looped over my shoulder, and rubbed her clit frantically, chasing her release. She would come on my cock, and soon after, I would make her come with my mouth.

Again and again.

She wanted to find her friends. I knew this, but I wanted my fill of her first.

As if I could ever get enough of her.

S'mara came and clenched so hard around me that my thrusts were interrupted, and I snarled, gripped her hips harder, and used her to fuck me. Her moans were replaced with squeals and screams as I came, pumping my seed deep into her and not pulling out, only tugging her against me. S'mara released a heavy breath when her chest hit mine, and my cock twitched inside her, making her moan again.

"I'll never be weak around you again, S'mara. I'll take care of you."

She rested her chin on my shoulder, reached her arms around, and traced circles across my back with her delicate fingers. "It's okay if you are... we can be stronger together."

I pulled her closer, wrapped my arms around her, and held her against my chest.

Stronger together.

I liked that.

CHAPTER 25

SAMARA

Lanir watched me more than he watched where we were going. He watched me *so intently* whenever I asked a question or answered one of his. I'd catch him staring at me if I looked away to take in the scenery or an unusual plant.

"Why do you keep looking at me?" I asked, and I could feel my cheeks as they flushed pink.

"To remind myself you're here with me."

I squeezed his hand, my chest swelling with emotion. There were so many layers to this being— more than I could have ever predicted. "I'm not going anywhere, Lanir." He huffed out a breath before the growling started in his chest. Without another word, he bent and scooped me into his arms, ignoring my squeal of surprise. "What are you doing?"

"We're going to find your friends."

I cried out again as he bolted, moving across the landscape too fast for me to appreciate the changing environment as we headed back toward the mountains. It seemed now Lanir was comfortable that I wasn't going anywhere, so he was happier to help me find the other girls. Was he so concerned I would simply leave him the moment I found them? At this point, I knew Lanir better than I knew them. Sure, they were my friends because of what we'd been through, and it was important I knew they were okay, but as for what happened after that, we could figure it out together. All I knew was I didn't want to let Lanir go. I wanted to let our connection grow and flourish. I wanted him to teach me all about this planet.

I wanted to build a life with him.

The thought startled me, but what else could I do? Lanir had explained the planet was closed off from intergalactic travel due to the Ghaal's actions. Other than pirates, there was no way to get home, and I had nothing to offer as payment. Chances are they'd see me as more valuable cargo than any payment anyway and sell me to the highest bidder, perhaps even back into the hands of the Ghaal.

So I sought the positive, and that was I had somehow landed on my feet here. I'd found someone—a male for me—I connected with on a level I'd never experienced before. I'd given myself to him, physically and emotionally, and once I knew the others were safe, there was nothing left to do but be together.

We could do anything.

I curled into Lanir's arms as he ran, unhindered by my weight or the supplies he carried, his spear banging against his shoulder where it was slung over with a loop of leather. The scenery whooshed past and made my head spin, so instead, I focused on something closer—Lanir's skin and the deep charcoal gray coloring of it with those red lines dappled through, looking dangerous like fire.

But I knew what lay underneath.

I traced my fingers across the lines. There was no difference in texture between the oranges and reds and grays and blacks, and after a moment, his chest rumbled with another growl.

"Careful, S'mara..."

It was the same warning he'd given me the last time I teased him, and I smirked, feeling bold and leaning against him to run my tongue over the salty sweat on his chest. He snarled this time, and his arms tightened around me.

"Are you trying to distract me?"

"I don't have to try very hard," I said, holding back a giggle.

Lanir huffed out a breath again, but his lips were curved into a smirk, and I simply sighed and leaned against him, letting him carry me back to the mountains.

"Tell me again why we need to do this." I squirmed under Lanir's touch, wiggling my nose as his fingers crossed my cheeks.

"You're too pale… you need to camouflage."

"But war paint?"

His fingers paused on my cheek, and his eyes darted to mine. "We're not at war."

I held his gaze, and my smile dropped. There was something behind his look like he was at war again, and I wondered what he was thinking.

It was as if he was holding back the words, *not yet.*

But he would tell me.

He always did when he was ready.

"It's just what we called it back on Earth."

Lanir resumed painting my skin. He'd crumbled some of the dark rock and mixed it with the juices from the same plant he'd used to heal my belly button when the piercing tore out, creating a paint. He'd streaked it across my face and arms, designed to help me blend against the rock before we headed to Ilk's.

Just in case, Lanir had said.

Just in case Lanir's brother, Ilk, failed to rescue one of the other girls and the Ghaal were around.

The words he didn't say made my skin crawl.

I sat still and let Lanir work, certain he was taking longer than necessary, partially because he liked touching me and partially to delay the inevitable—when we're no longer alone with just each other.

"I feel like a warrior princess."

"Do you want to be a warrior princess?" Lanir asked the question with such sincerity I burst out laughing, and he pulled his fingers away from my face, his lips curling into a smirk.

"Yes. Yes, I do want to be one."

He moved in to resume his painting but stopped with his lips inches from mine. "Then you're my warrior princess."

I sucked in a breath, unable to tell if he was being intentionally sensual or not. I jolted forward to kiss his lips quickly and giggled at how his smirk fell away to be replaced with surprise. Every time I touched him with affection when I took his hand or brushed my fingers over his arm, there was still a moment when he was surprised—a delayed reaction where, in that split second, he couldn't comprehend someone touching him with anything other than violence.

I knew it would take time, but I smiled because we *had* the time. All the time in the world until he realized I wouldn't hurt him, and I trusted him to protect me.

We were stronger together.

EPILOGUE

SAMARA

Coming around the side of the mountain and seeing Erica, I couldn't describe the feeling.

Lanir had gently shoved me against the rocks and moved ahead when he heard something, and I followed when a female's voice carried to me.

One of the girls, they were *safe*.

"Samara, oh my God!"

She ran toward me, and I stumbled over a few rocks as I ran to meet her halfway. When Erica threw her arms around me, after a moment, she tensed. I opened my eyes to see her staring over my shoulder. Craning my neck, Lanir was inches behind us, his teeth bared and looking every part the demon I thought he was when I first saw him.

"It's okay," I muttered to Erica, pulling away from the hug and resting my hands on her arms as though I needed to convince myself she was really alive and safe. "This is Lanir, Ilk's brother."

Erica's eyes flickered to mine before shifting back to Lanir. "We've met. He said you were leaving the mountains."

I glanced at Lanir, understanding immediately. His posture was tense as he watched Erica and Ilk. He was trying so hard to be comfortable and still, but being near his brother must be surfacing the memories again. Erica was safe, and now we knew that, he was ready to leave again.

I nodded. "Yes, we will. But I think we need to spend some time together and make a plan."

"We came looking for you," Erica said, and rubbed my arm gently.

Ilk strode up behind Erica, his casual gait in stark contrast to Lanir's possessive lean, but the way Ilk rested his hand on Erica's lower back was more than enough to tell he was just as protective over her as Lanir was of me. I thrust my hand out, an internal voice screaming, surprised I made such a bold move when mere weeks ago I would have shrunk away at the idea of introducing myself to a stranger.

Let alone a strange alien.

But my previous social anxieties seemed to pale in comparison to what I'd experienced recently, to what I had proven to myself I was capable of. Ilk took my hand, his fingers gently gripping mine, and I noted the porous feel of his skin as if he was also made of the mountain. Once we'd moved away from where the lava pits dotted the side of the mountain, the color had slowly changed from charcoal to a gray dappled with purple. Ilk's skin was this color, adapted to blend into his environment as Lanir had with his. Their facial features were similar, though Ilk had a friendlier, more open face. I wondered if, despite their adaptations, they would keep the elements of their face that made it their own if they changed again.

Another thing I'd need to ask Lanir.

Ilk released my hand and looked over the top of my head to his brother. "Lanir, it's good to see you."

Lanir simply grunted, and I pressed my lips together. I knew Lanir was happy to see his brother, but this wasn't easy for him. He was still plagued with fear about the weaknesses he thought he had, and he didn't trust himself. Lanir brought forth all the anger inside him to help him control everything he could, constantly trying to make up for the weakness he felt he contained.

The anger helped him.

I knew all this now.

I knew the being behind me better than I'd known anyone, and I just hoped Ilk understood without Lanir having to explain again. Erica was watching Lanir wearily, and I patted her arm, bringing her attention back to me and smiling to reassure her.

My smile dropped. "The others, have you found any of them?"

"We found Tori. She landed in the forest and is with Vitri."

Lanir stiffened behind me at Vitri's name, and I stepped back to place a hand on his arm and squeeze slightly to tell him without words that *everything was okay.*

"Misha?"

Erica wrung her hands together. "We don't know yet. We came around this way to find Lanir and see if he'd gotten to a pod. I didn't know if I was going to find you or Misha. Tori and Vitri are on their way to the beach to find Sahcor, so hopefully, he has found Misha, and she's safe too."

"He'll have found her. I'm sure she's okay."

Erica held my eye contact, trying to force a smile that didn't quite work. I *had* to believe Misha was okay. If Sahcor found her, and she was, we could all come together and figure out how we wanted to live. Maybe together as a big community. Maybe our presence would stop Lanir or his brothers from changing to breed. Did it even work that way? I didn't know.

Misha had to be okay. If Sahcor were anything like his brothers, he would have found and protected her.

We reached Ilk's cave within a few hours, and I was grateful there was food and water for us.

"Just wait until you see the hot springs," Erica said. She seemed happy, but I could tell from the slight furrow in her brow she wouldn't be able to truly relax until we knew Misha was okay. I wouldn't either.

I smiled. "I've seen them. We have them near Lanir's place too."

"Oh, cool. I think the plan is to wait here until Tori and Vitri come back, right, Ilk?"

There was no answer, and we turned.

Ilk and Lanir were staring each other down, standing face to face and chest to chest. Lanir's hands were curled into fists at his sides.

Lanir broke the silence, his voice thick and gravelly, his eyes straying from Ilk's to look at me every other moment. "We need a war, Ilk. I don't care what you say, we need to take down the Ghaal. Your hatred for violence has held us back, and they *must* be stopped. We can't fear their retaliation, as they strike regardless of our actions. We should have ended it a long time ago."

"I know." The resignation was heavy in Ilk's tone, and Lanir's brows drew together.

"You know?"

"You're right. I should've listened long ago. I guess it took me having something to lose..." He looked at Erica, and her expression softened, full of affection and perhaps even love. I glanced back and forth between Erica and Ilk, almost *feeling* their connection through the air. Turning, I found Lanir staring at me, his expression darkened after his conversation with Ilk, but always telling me the same thing without words.

I'll protect you.

I offered him a smile, and his lip twitched in response.

To break the tension, I pointed to Erica. "See, Lanir? She gets her own spear."

Lanir snarled, and Erica jumped, making me laugh. "I'll make you a spear," he growled out the words, harsh and grating, and Erica's eyes widened.

I patted her arm, still laughing, and felt her muscles relax under my touch.

He may look like a demon, but there was so much more to him than met the eye.

And he was *mine.*

I couldn't help but smile.

We waited by Ilk's cave for almost two days, working together to gather food supplies, making extra clothes and water bags, and keeping them filled. We bathed together, and while I wasn't keen on being naked around others, I was eventually able to relax in Erica's company, although she had to keep slapping Ilk's hands away when he tried to wash her even in front of me, and her cheeks would flame.

We were gathering wood for a fire when Lanir stopped, sniffing the air. I moved to him and touched his arm, but he didn't look down. Instead, he tilted his head toward the woodlands in the distance.

"Vitri is near." He sniffed again as Ilk came to his side. "And a human."

Erica was at my side, her grip on my arm almost painful. "A human? As in *one?*"

Lanir snarled. "One Synth. One human." He turned to me, grabbed my arm, and swung me over his back. "Come."

I wrapped my arms around his neck as he took off and turned back to see Ilk put his arm protectively around Erica as she wrapped her arms around her chest.

There had to be a mistake. Maybe humans' scent isn't as strong as Synths, and he didn't pick up one of the girls?

Oh, please let Misha be safe.

Lanir skidded to an abrupt stop as a female voice shouted, "Stop *right* there!"

My shock subsided to a quiet giggle I couldn't help despite the situation. I didn't know Tori well, but well enough to know it was her as she said, "I've had just about enough of being attacked by every single one of Vitri's damn brothers. If you are who I think you are, you can introduce yourself in a civilized manner."

Lanir snarled before he reached back and lifted me over his shoulder before he placed me on my feet. I stood for a moment. The feeling of walking away from Lanir didn't occur to me until he nudged me slightly toward Tori.

Because he trusted me to come back to him.

I smiled, flicking my hair out of my face, and ran the final distance to Tori, pulling her into a tight hug with her arms clamped to her sides. Tori laughed, her body relaxed, and she patted my back awkwardly.

When I pulled back, I took her in. "Wow, Tori, I love your hair."

She smirked. "You look amazing." She paused before she pulled me in for another hug, a proper one where her arms weren't pinned, and I smiled against her shoulder. A growl came from Lanir, and Tori tensed again.

"Easy, Lanir, she means no harm," the other Synth, who I assumed to be Vitri, said, then he spoke in their native tongue. Lanir's eyes flickered to Tori, but only briefly before settling on me again, and his expression softened.

"Where's Misha?" I asked, looking behind Tori for someone else.

"On her way."

I nodded as Lanir stared at Vitri, the air between them electric and tense.

"We're making a plan," Lanir grunted out, holding out his hand for me. "Come." I took his hand and followed him as we made our way back to Ilk's, Vitri and Tori following slowly behind.

The tension between Lanir and Vitri was still thick in the air back at the cave, though you wouldn't be able to tell from the carefree smile on Vitri's face whenever he looked at Tori. Lanir circled wherever Vitri stood like a cat or a boxer before a fight.

He was worried about what they thought of him.

But I was worried about Misha.

She and Sahcor weren't with Tori and Vitri as I had expected them to be. Tori had said they would be joining us soon, but I hovered around nervously as Tori and Erica embraced again, wringing my hands together, waiting for a break in their safety checks so I could ask questions.

When there was no natural lull in the conversation, I finally snapped. "Where is Misha?" The words came out harsher than I had intended.

Tori rounded on me, and from the little I knew about her, I expected her to tell me off for interrupting them. Instead, she threw a glance at Vitri—a green Synth who looked to be made of moss and vines—before she looked back at me.

"She ran away when we tried to bring her back."

Erica grabbed Tori's shoulder. "Why would she do that?"

Tori let out a shuddering breath. It was unsettling to see her this bothered. She always fought on the spaceship when we were taken—she fought every step of the way. But watching her now, her eyes swam with concern, and it made my chest constrict with worry.

"She'd been previously taken by the Ghaal and had some sort of tag implanted in her arm."

A thunderous growl rumbled out from behind me, and I turned to see Ilk and Lanir with matching expressions of rage twisted on their faces.

Tori hesitated, speaking again only when Vitri lay a comforting hand on her shoulder. "It started flashing when I got near her, and she ran away, saying they'll use her to find us. Sahcor went after her and told us to go ahead, and they'd catch up."

I opened my mouth to speak, and Tori held up a hand. "There's something else Misha said." She directed her attention to Vitri and Ilk. "She said there were others... other human women."

"That's impossible." Ilk's voice was thick with

emotion, but the slight shift of his gaze to Lanir betrayed his uncertainty. "They're all dead."

"Apparently not," Tori said, holding Ilk's stare when Lanir wouldn't look at her.

"Where is Sahcor? Where is Misha?" I asked, twisting my hands together. Repeating the same questions wouldn't change the answer, but I couldn't help myself. This didn't feel right. We were all meant to come together and then decide what to do. "We all need to be together. Everyone needs to be safe, then we can figure out how to help the others."

"Sahcor won't be far behind us," Vitri said.

The tightening in my chest constricted further. *Something felt wrong.* "How can you be sure?"

Vitri threw a glance at me, not accusing or angry for my questioning, but worry blossomed in his eyes. We all knew, but no one was saying it. It wouldn't have taken Sahcor that long to catch up with Misha since the Synths were faster than us. They should've been right behind them.

Something was wrong.

The next few hours passed slowly, time an agonizing drag as the sun almost finished its curve across the sky without a sign of Sahcor or Misha. We continued to work on gathering supplies, but there was only so much we could do. Conversation was difficult to maintain, and although I'm sure Tori and Erica had as many unanswered questions as I did about this planet, nothing seemed particularly important right now. Nothing else really mattered until Misha was here, and we were all together.

But I kept thinking about what Tori said about Misha's concerns that the Ghaal would use her to find us.

What if she wasn't here because she didn't *want* to be?

The days passed fairly uneventful, which, given everything that had happened, would have been a good thing if it weren't for the one event we were waiting for—Misha's return.

Lanir came up behind me as I sat with the girls, and I immediately stood to face him. He'd been keeping his distance from his brothers, and I had to keep reminding him that I was sure they would understand why. They, better than anyone, in fact. They'd witnessed his suffering and the way he was broken down into an animal. Thankfully, his brothers didn't push him Dand let him stalk the perimeter of the area, never far enough away that I couldn't see him.

But still, Lanir had been the first to leap at the chance to go meet Eldich, who lived in the woodlands beyond Lanir's cave, past the area with the sandy floors and those horrible little creatures that almost took Lanir away from me.

I gripped his arm. "Please be careful. Are you sure you don't want me to come with you?"

His fingers traced my face, and a tingle ran up my spine. Tori and Erica were still weary of Lanir, and while I wanted them to understand him the way I did, selfishly a part of me *didn't* want them to understand. Because I wanted him all to myself and for this bond we held to be between only us.

"I do want you with me," he murmured, keeping his voice low like he also wanted what was between us to stay between us. "But I will move faster alone."

"Afraid I'll distract you?" I teased and brushed my fingers over his chest, ending with a flick, displaying confidence in flirting I'd *never* had before. But I could be myself with Lanir, and something about his stoic nature only made me want to make him smile more.

His lip twitched, and he leaned down, crowding my space with his body. His lips were a whisper away from my ear when he growled out, "When I return, I'll sneak you away from everyone and fuck you until you scream my name."

My thighs clenched together as I was left momentarily wordless. "Be careful," I whispered.

He pressed his lips to my forehead. "I'll return soon."

He thundered away, leaping over rocks I would have scrambled to get around. I knew he was right about moving faster without me, but my chest ached from the moment he disappeared from my sight.

Erica approached me and placed a hand on my shoulder, also watching the space where Lanir had gone. "He'll be back soon, Samara. He's only going to tell Eldich we're gathering, then he'll be back. Eldich will be the one to make the trip out farther to bring back Ryth."

I nodded, reached up, and gripped her fingers in mine, afraid if I opened my mouth to respond, I would cry.

Lanir was back in under two days, and I ran to meet him, but I tripped over the boulders and scraped my leg. He snarled when he realized I was hurting myself to get to him, and he sped up, closing the distance between us, and scooped me up in his arms.

"You hurt yourself," he snarled out.

"I missed you."

He huffed out an angry breath from his nose as if that was no excuse and returned me to the group before putting me back on my feet.

We kept waiting.

Lanir settled back into the group, and as was his way, he sat apart from the others on the outskirts of the flat area in front of Ilk's cave before the rocks turned large and sharp. I sat between Lanir's legs and rested my back against his chest, watching his hands as he sharpened a spear for me using a bone knife.

When he paused his movements, I felt the growl rumble through him, and I looked up at him. He reached to brush my cheek, and I sniffled, hastily wiping my face. I didn't realize I had shed a tear.

"You're crying."

I released a small chuckle. "Sorry, I was just thinking about Misha and these other girls we don't even know. Hoping they're safe…"

He growled again, and I turned to press my ear against the rumbling of his chest, sighing against the soothing vibrations and letting the sound surround me. It wasn't aggressive, not toward me. The growl was protective and possessive, creating a cage of safety as I snuggled into his arms when Lanir abandoned his work to hold me close.

"I love you," I whispered, taking in a sharp breath when I realized what I'd said.

Would he understand the significance of the words?

"I love you too, S'mara," he rumbled out,

brushing my hair with a gentleness that never ceased to make me smile, given his size. "We'll all be together and safe soon."

"I know." And I did. I believed him.

Once everyone was safe and well, all I wanted to do was be with Lanir.

Together.

Stronger together.

Continue with…
Liberator – Elements of Abduction Book 4
for
Misha and Sahcor's story

Misha and Sahcor are on the run from the Ghaal,
but will a close call lead to re-capture?

ACKNOWLEDGMENTS

There is something so satisfying about the grumpy/sunshine trope, isn't there? It's right up there with enemies to lovers as one of my favorites.

I hope you loved Book Three in the *Elements of Abduction* novels.

I'd like to take this chance to thank you, my readers. Putting a book out there that is essentially a piece of your soul is a big thing, and every kind word I get is such a boost. Please leave a review—they're so important to indie authors, and we appreciate every one of them.

Again, thank you.

You're amazing, and I look forward to bringing you more stories!

ANGELS AND FIRE BOOKS

Find our exciting stories at:

www.angelsandfirebooks.com.au

READER GROUP

Want access to fun, prizes and sneak peeks?

Stefanie Dawn

Join my Facebook Reader Group.
https://www.facebook.com/groups/588038442170571

NEWSLETTER

Sign up for my Newsletter.
https://www.subscribepage.com/angelsandfirebooks

BOOKBUB

https://www.bookbub.com/authors/stefanie-dawn

GOODREADS

Add my books to your TBR list
on my Goodreads profile.
https://www.goodreads.com/author/
show/21761217.Stefanie_Dawn

AMAZON

https://www.amazon.com/author/stefaniedawn

WEBSITE

http://www.angelsandfirebooks.com.au/

INSTAGRAM

https://www.instagram.com/angelsandfirebooks

EMAIL

info@angelsandfirebooks.com.au

FACEBOOK

https://www.facebook.com/stefaniedawnwriter

ABOUT THE AUTHOR

Stefanie Dawn has been a writer and creative soul all her life **and** strives to give her readers stories they can escape into as they become absorbed in the worlds created.

When she isn't writing, Stefanie might be painting, reading, or watching movies. She loves the process of producing films as another form of storytelling. There's also a good chance she'll be baking some delicious treats—pretending she won't later regret consuming them—or simply enjoying a cocktail with friends.

Stefanie Dawn lives in South Australia with her ever-supportive partner and a lovable gang of rescue cats.

You can stay up to date with
Stefanie and her books at:
www.angelsandfirebooks.com.au

www.ingramcontent.com/pod-product-compliance
Lightning Source LLC
Chambersburg PA
CBHW051142190726
48290CB00006B/1955